Jerry Raine
was born in Yorkshire and ⬚⬚⬚⬚⬚⬚
the age of sixteen, he mov⬚⬚⬚⬚⬚
he worked as a farmhand a⬚⬚ ⬚⬚avan-fitter, and
made his singing début in some of Sydney's seed-
ier bars. Returning to England, he worked in a
variety of jobs until the age of forty-one, when his
first novel, *Smalltime*, was published by The Do-
Not Press. *Small Change* is a sequel to *Smalltime*,
and in between he wrote a couple more for a
larger publisher. As a singer-songwriter, Jerry has
shared the stage with Iris DeMent, Christy
Moore, Steve Forbert, Gretchen Peters and
others.

Small Change

Jerry Raine

First Published in Great Britain in 2001 by
The Do-Not Press Limited
16 The Woodlands
London SE13 6TY

Casebound edition: ISBN 1 899 344 74 8
B-format paperback: ISBN 1 899344 75 6

British Library Cataloguing in Publication Data. A catalogue
record for this book is available from the British Library.

h g f e d c b a

Printed and bound in Great Britain by
The Guernsey Press Co Ltd.

For their help at various stages of my writing career I would like to thank the following: Simon Brett, Michael Motley, Maxim Jakubowski, Jim Driver, Ian Rankin, Mike Petty, Thomas Wortche and Ion Mills.

Most of all I would like to thank Pam Smith, my best friend and agent, who died on April 24th 2000. Without Pam's belief and encouragement I would have given up writing a long time ago. Somehow I made it to the fourth book, though she never had the chance to read it. Pam was a shining light who inspired many people. She changed my life and will always be with me.

For their help with this book, thanks are due to Tabitha Morris and Debbie Epstein.

Dedicated with love to the memory of Pam Smith.
1955-2000

1

WHEN CHRIS SMALL came home from work on Friday evening, there was a large policeman standing outside his gate. He was at least six foot four and was staring at the pub over the road, no doubt wishing he could have a pint. It was nearly ten o'clock and Chris was thinking about having a pint too, but instead he walked over and said, 'Evening all.'

The policeman looked at him with a scowl and said, 'I haven't heard that one before.'

'Sorry,' Chris said. 'I live here. Can I squeeze through?'

The policeman stepped away from the entrance to Chris's lodgings, a rickety brown gate between two brick walls, and said, 'Well you'd better go up then. There's been a robbery.'

Chris felt his stomach turn. 'What kind of robbery?'

The policeman looked at him as if he were an idiot. 'The kind where they take things.'

Chris decided not to pursue the matter and walked quickly up the cement steps that led to the front door. It was wide open and one of the other lodgers was standing there with his girl-friend. 'What's going on?' Chris asked him.

'We've been bloody robbed,' the lodger said.

Chris had never found out his name. He was a skinny, unwell-looking kid in his early twenties, who always wore jeans and a leather jacket. He was also a heavy metal freak and rented the room below Chris's. He often played loud music that thumped through the floor and he had long dirty hair and a permanent lump high on his left cheek.

'You mean all of us?' Chris asked.

'Well I have. You'd better go and check your room.'

Chris squeezed past them, nodding at the girlfriend. She also had long dirty hair and wore a leather jacket, but unlike her boyfriend, she was on the plump side.

Chris walked down the linoleum-floored corridor past the bathroom, then turned left up the flight of stairs that led to the first small landing. John, a middle-aged bus driver, was standing outside his room. He nodded at Chris and said, 'They got my stereo, the sods.' He looked as if he were about to burst into tears. He was a lover of country music and spent long hours in his room, listening to records. Conway Twitty and Tammy Wynette.

Chris poked his head around the door and looked in. 'Well at least they didn't take your records.' He could see stacks of them sitting on the floor.

'No one's interested in vinyl these days,' John said. 'One of the saving graces of the LP is that nobody wants to nick them.'

Chris smiled. He was glad to see John hadn't lost his sense of humour. He patted him on the shoulder. 'I'll go and see what my room's like.'

He stepped up to the next landing, walked past the vacant room on his left, and pushed open his door at the end of the corridor. Inside he found a policeman looking out of the window at Elmhurst High Street. 'Nice view?' Chris asked, and the policeman jumped with surprise and turned around.

'Not bad,' said the policeman. 'If they cut away a bit of the tree out there.'

'Yeah, I don't know who's responsible for that.'

'The council, probably.'

There was a tree growing from the pavement below that was starting to obscure Chris's only window. He didn't mind too much, though, because he didn't plan on living there forever. He looked around the room and saw straight away what was missing.

'Shit!' he said.

'Pardon me?' said the policeman.

'My stereo's gone, and my TV and video. And none of it was insured.' Chris slumped on to the bed and watched the policeman get out his notebook. He pulled up one of Chris's matching two chairs, thin white metal with a hard seat, and took down Chris's details. He was a big man with a friendly, red face.

'How long have you lived here?' he asked.

'Two years. Obviously one day too long.'

'Is anything else missing?'

Chris glanced around. 'No. There's not much room for anything else.'

His room had pink walls, a single bed, a white metal table to match the chairs, a portable gas heater, and one wardrobe. There was also a crappy old fridge where he kept a pint of milk and one week's food.

'And how much were the stolen belongings worth?' asked the policeman.

Chris knew exactly how much they were worth because he'd only bought them about a month ago. He'd thrown out all his old gear and purchased the new appliances on his Visa, at Dixons in Bromley. He'd caught a black cab home with the three boxes loaded in next to him. 'The TV was £260. The video was £150, and the stereo was £500. £910 altogether.'

The policeman wrote the figures down. 'Well, maybe they saw you bringing them in. That's what often happens. They see you unloading and it sets their minds working. Either that or they see the empty boxes down by the bins. Did you leave the boxes down there?'

'Yeah. Where else am I going to put them in a room this size?'

'It's best to conceal them if you can. Break them up. Stick them in a black bin bag. It happens all the time.'

'I'll make a mental note of it,' Chris said bitterly. 'But what about the other rooms? How did they manage to do them all?'

'Just bad luck,' the policeman said. 'Probably did yours first then the others on the way out. Three lodgers and none of you were in. What about that room next door?'

'That's been empty for a while.' The last tenant had been a mad alcoholic, prone to midnight fits. He would throw furniture around the room and rant and rave. Thankfully, the land-lord had thrown him out after a few weeks.

The policeman looked at his notebook. 'And the landlord's a Mr Packard?'

'Yeah, he lives in Spain. His ex-wife collects the rent.'

The policeman nodded. 'There's been a lot of this going on recently. Sometimes a gang will hit a town, do several robberies, then move on when they're finished.'

'Great,' Chris said sarcastically. Was that meant to make him feel better?

The policeman stood up. 'Well, that's all I need for now. We'll check out the usual villains and let you know. I doubt if you'll get your stuff back though.'

'I didn't think I would.'

'And I should get the landlord's wife to fix a stronger lock on the front door. That one was forced open with hardly any effort.'

'Right.'

'If you need me, just ask at the station. My name's Larry Williamson.' He reached in his pocket, brought out a business card, and handed it to Chris.

Chris was amazed. Did policemen have business cards these days? 'Okay, thanks,' he said.

He watched him leave then put his head in his hands. He had been looking forward to watching '*Frasier*' on TV, his usual Friday night viewing. Now what would he do? He glanced at his shelves and noticed that his dozen or so CDs had also gone, including the latest Mark Eitzel that he'd only bought a few days ago. He swore. It was only a small collec-tion but he'd been having fun buying new music after throw-ing out all his vinyl and cassettes.

Then he remembered his only other expensive electrical item, one he had totally forgotten about. He stepped over to the wardrobe and opened the door, then bent down and lifted a pile of T-shirts and jumpers off the bottom. He breathed a sigh of relief; it was still there.

It was a laptop computer that he'd bought several years ago with the intention of playing computer games. It was worth over a thousand pounds but he'd soon grown weary of it, not having the patience to learn more than about five per cent of its capabilities. Still, he was glad the thieves hadn't got their dirty little hands on it. He covered it back up with the clothes then sat down on the bed and thought of the weeks ahead. What the hell was he going to do in his spare time without a TV and stereo? He couldn't afford to go and buy another set. He was a victim of crime for the second time in his life, and it was a feeling he didn't particularly care for.

2

THE NEXT MORNING Chris went to work as usual, leaving the house just after eight. It was dull and overcast outside, which summed up the way he felt. He hated working on Saturdays when the rest of the world was lying in. When was the last time he'd had a weekend off? He couldn't remember.

He was working six days a week on his own, in a privately owned off-licence called Rowan's in Lambs Conduit Street in London, his only day off being Monday. It was getting him down working so many hours and he was trying to persuade his boss, Rowan, to take on a Sunday part-timer so at least he could have a two-day break. But Rowan, like most bosses Chris had worked for, was tight-fisted, and didn't trust any newcomers. Chris felt he was doomed to working alone until Rowan regained his health.

Six months ago, Rowan had suffered a stroke and now only came to the shop to pick up bottles of wine (he had been told to give up whisky by his doctor), so Chris's only companion was the radio. He didn't mind that too much as Rowan was a bit of an oddball, but sometimes he felt his life was drifting by without any human contact at all. Apart from the customers, who were only interested in small talk, he didn't speak to anyone all day. He couldn't remember the last time he'd had a decent conversation or even laughed out loud at something. Things would have to change soon or he'd surely go mad or start talking to himself.

As he walked towards Elmhurst station, Chris was still seething about the previous night's losses. Without a TV and stereo he felt he would go stir-crazy in his little room, with even more silence than usual to contend with. The only positive thing about the robbery was that Mr Heavy Metal underneath had also had his stereo nicked, so there would be no head banging music coming through the floorboards for a while. Chris hoped Heavy Metal was going a little stir-crazy too, but at least he had a girlfriend to keep him occupied.

Stir-crazy.

Chris had first heard the term in an Eagles song way back in the seventies. It was in a song called 'Doolin, Dalton' on their second, and best, album, *Desperado*. There was another song on it called 'Twenty-One', all about the exuberance of youth, and Chris could remember singing along to it on his car stereo, wondering what it would be like to reach such a ripe old age. Now, without too much blinking, he had suddenly reached the age of thirty-nine and would be reaching the dreaded forty next year.

So what exactly had he achieved in his life this far? It was a conversation he had with himself nearly every waking moment, and his life achievements could be listed as follows:

1. He had about a thousand pounds tucked away in a building society for emergencies;

2. He had a job, albeit yet another one without any long-term prospects; and

3. He was still alive.

He supposed the last point was the most important, but if he wasn't really living his life, was there much point in still being around? Could he really face another thirty-five years of going through the motions? He knew he had to get rid of such negative thoughts, but how? Maybe a new girlfriend would do the trick, but that was easier said than done; he hadn't been out with anyone for nearly a year.

It was an eighteen-minute walk to the station and the last hundred yards were down a steep hill. Chris let the momentum carry him along until he was almost running. Coming home in the evening it was a tougher walk; he had to trudge up the hill, and it was always very tiring after a long day. The exercise kept him fairly fit though because, with the walk at the London end added on, he reckoned he was doing about five miles a day. It certainly helped to keep him trim.

At the station he bought a newspaper and walked through the piss-smelling tunnel beneath the tracks. Emerging on platform two, he sat on a bench and scanned the front page but, seeing there were no disasters in the world, turned to the back page instead. After a few minutes of taking nothing in, he looked at the trees that grew high above the platforms.

Elmhurst was a pleasant part of suburbia in which to live, and Chris didn't mind commuting everyday into London, as it was only a thirty-minute ride into Charing Cross. It was almost like living in the country, and in a way, he thought he had the best of both worlds: he could be entertained in the dirty city at night, and then escape to the clean suburbs afterwards. Yes, Elmhurst was an okay kind of place to live – he could just do with a little excitement to liven things up.

His train arrived on time about five minutes later, and he stepped through the sliding doors. It was still too early for most shoppers to be travelling into town, so he found an empty bay of seats and sat down.

As the train pulled away, Chris spread the newspaper on his lap and took a small pack of cards from his jacket. He had found them in a drawer last night and played a few games of patience before going to bed. The cards had helped to drain his tension away because he was forced to think about something else. He had read somewhere that this was a common trait in men; to unwind they needed to do something of a practical or problem-solving nature like DIY or fixing their car, whereas women would more readily talk about their hang-ups. Chris hated cars and DIY though, so cards were a good alternative at the moment.

As he played, Chris sensed someone looking at him, and when he glanced up, he saw a fair-haired girl a few seats away staring. He looked back down at the cards, played a few more minutes, then looked back up. She was still staring so he nodded and smiled, and much to his surprise she stood up, came over and sat down opposite.

'I saw you playing,' she said with a smile. 'I like to play cards as well.'

'Oh yeah?' Chris said. 'What do you play?'

'Blackjack.'

'Okay.' Chris scooped the cards from the newspaper, shuffled them quickly and looked at the girl. 'What shall we play for?'

She reached in her coat pocket and took out a box of matches. 'We'll have twenty each and see who wins.'

'You're on,' Chris said, and watched while she counted them out.

She was dressed all in black: slacks, pullover and thin jacket. Her hair came down just below her ears in a boyish style, and she had a pixie face with thin lips, almost no cheekbones. Chris watched as she reached over with a handful of matches and placed them on his newspaper. On her own lap she spread a carrier bag, and counted twenty matches for herself.

'Ready?' Chris asked. 'I'll be banker.' Then he started dealing.

It only took him a few hands to realise that the girl in front of him knew exactly what she was doing. Chris hadn't played blackjack for years, couldn't remember the finer rules of it, and soon she was spiriting the matches off his newspaper and over to her carrier. She smiled when she won and looked very serious when she didn't.

'Do you play regularly?' he asked between hands.

'Quite regularly,' she said.

'My name's Chris, by the way.'

'Mine's Edie.'

'Where do you play?'

'Casinos,' Edie said, nonchalantly.

Chris dealt some more, now knowing he was playing someone who took it quite seriously. She played in casinos. Who was this strange girl?

It only took another five minutes and all of Chris's matches were gone. He smiled at Edie and said, 'You play very well.'

'Thanks. But you'll have to learn some basic rules. Your game is obviously a little rusty.'

'I haven't played for a long time. I've never learnt it properly.'

'I can see that,' she laughed.

Chris decided to take a chance. 'Maybe you could teach me how.'

Edie looked at him warily and then smiled. 'Maybe I could.'

'Another game?'

'Okay.'

Chris watched again as she counted out the matches. She had nice long slim fingers, no rings.

They joked a bit as they played and as the train filled up around them several people started watching. Chris wished the train journey was a little longer but soon they were approaching Charing Cross. He had managed to win a few hands this time but knew it was more down to luck than skill. And Edie still had the majority of the matches.

'So what are you coming into London for. Shopping?' she asked, as the train pulled into the station.

Chris packed up the cards and put them back in his jacket. 'I work up here. How about you?'

'Work as well. If you'd like a cheap meal why don't you come and see me later?'

Chris was amazed at the invitation. 'Where do you work?' he asked.

'You know the Trocadero?' Edie said. 'There's a restaurant there called Mario's. I'm a waitress. I'll be working until eight.'

'I know where it is,' Chris said. 'I don't finish till eight either, though. It'll take me half an hour to walk there.'

'I'll wait in the coffee bar.'

They left the carriage together and walked down the platform. Edie was only a few inches shorter than Chris, probably about five-eight, and he guessed she was about twenty-five. It felt good walking beside her and he thought back to an hour ago, and how depressed he'd been feeling. Now, all those thoughts had been banished from his mind. Maybe the excitement he needed in his life was about to begin.

When they reached the station concourse he shook Edie's hand and said, 'See you later'.

She smiled and they headed off in different directions.

3

TWENTY-FIVE MINUTES later Chris arrived at the off-licence, a walk he could almost do in his sleep. A few other shops were already open, like the Indian supermarket, the newsagents, and the greengrocers. There were the usual black rubbish sacks lying on the pavement outside other shops, awaiting collection by the binmen during the week. He stood outside the front door and searched in his pocket for the keys. The woodwork around the windows of Rowan's was painted dark green, a colour Chris normally associated with gardening shops. The letters of the sign above were painted, unimaginatively, in white. The front door was in-between two windows, one holding a display for beer and spirits, the other an arrangement of wine. Chris changed the displays when he became bored with looking at them, or when the bottles were looking dusty or the labels faded by the sun.

He unlocked the front door, stepped inside and turned off the alarm, then walked to the back storeroom and office. In here there were cardboard boxes of overstocks, shrink-wrapped packets of mixers, a desk behind a one-way window, and a toilet and sink. Chris took off his coat and hung it on a chair, then started getting ready for the day.

At ten o'clock he opened the front door. He always liked opening on time, although it never made any difference because there was rarely anyone waiting. Then he sat behind the till and started reading the Saturday papers, intermittently staring off into space.

The floor of the off-licence was covered with old grey carpet showing stains where people had walked with muddy shoes, or spillage's from bottles of red wine from tastings held long ago. Chris vacuumed the place once a week, and dusted the shelves whenever he put out stock. The shelves covered three walls, while in the middle stood stacks of canned beer and bins of bestselling wine. New World wines were the most popular these days and any bottle with the magic word 'Chardonnay' on the label didn't hang around very long. Chris was often amused at how many customers considered themselves wine experts just because they knew the Chardonnay word, and felt frustrated that other bottles, which were just as good, were doomed to a life gathering dust.

Chris spent the rest of the day in a good mood as he thought about his forthcoming date, but wished he had put on some better clothes than the blue corduroys and grey jumper he was wearing. He chatted and joked with customers, listened to football commentary on the radio, and read the newspaper in-between. The takings topped the thousand-pound mark, which was always a good total to hit.

When eight o'clock rolled around Chris hid the money in a filing cabinet in the back room (Rowan was too stingy to buy a safe), set the alarm, and locked the shop behind him. He tried walking quickly to the Trocadero but the streets were too crowded. There seemed to be more people in London every year and he wondered when the whole place was going to grind to a halt. He found it immensely frustrating dodging tourists and traffic, and even more annoying, the many people who now cycled on the pavement. When had that suddenly become the thing to do? He could remember when he was a boy, growing up in Horley, when he'd been stopped and told off by a pensioner for cycling along a path next to a playing field. He had never cycled down it again. Now, all of a sudden, the London pavements were full of bicycle messengers and people cycling to work, and no one batted an eyelid. He couldn't figure it out. The quality of life was deteriorating.

Eventually he arrived at the Trocadero. He had sweat on his forehead and under his pullover. He stepped into the warm, bright, crowded shopping centre and took off his coat before he fainted. He walked over to Mario's – a smallish, brightly-lit restaurant on the main ground floor walkway – and found Edie sitting on a stool in the coffee bar. She waved at him and smiled.

'I didn't think you'd turn up,' she said.

'The offer of a free meal was too much,' he joked. 'But I was thinking. I know a quiet place in Leicester Square. Why don't we go there?'

A look of amazement came on Edie's face. 'There's a quiet place in Leicester Square? Is that possible?'

'I discovered it by chance once and every time I go back there's never anyone there.'

'Is the food really that bad?'

Chris laughed. 'No, it's pretty good actually.'

Edie slid from her stool and waved goodbye to a few of her colleagues. Chris followed her down the crowded walkway.

Chris had been in the Trocadero a few times before, but generally speaking, indoor shopping centres weren't his favourite places to visit. He still had bad memories about the one in Boroughheath and the time he'd got mixed up in a little shenanigans on the roof. The experience had nearly ruined his life, and it was something he still felt guilty about now and again. He had been avoiding shopping centres ever since.

The Trocadero had the usual mix of gift and clothes shops on the ground floor, then a three-screen cinema on the mezzanine, and an amusement arcade on the highest level. The arcade was very hot and sweaty, and far too noisy. Chris had wandered around it once and never been back. It had been full of spotty kids with vacant looks, and rucksacks on their backs.

They squeezed out of the front entrance, on to the busy street, then headed towards Leicester Square and Oscar's, the restaurant that Chris had discovered a few months ago. There was a café called Oscar's at the front, where people sat at tables under a large awning, and then a corridor beside it that led downstairs. Chris presumed the restaurant was quiet because no one ever thought of going down the corridor. It was lined with black-and-white photos of old film stars and he pointed them out as they descended. He was pleasantly surprised to find that Edie could name most of the actors.

'I like old films,' she explained. 'Working strange hours I tend to watch a lot during the daytime.'

Chris knew how true that was. When he'd been an aero-plane cleaner at Gatwick many years ago, he had spent many dead hours watching black-and-white films, waiting for his shifts to begin. Actually, back then, a black-and-white TV had been all he'd owned, so they were all black-and-white to him. It still caught him by surprise today when he watched a film and found that it had, in fact, been made in colour.

They came to two wooden doors and pulled them open. Inside, Oscar's was once again deserted, just two waitresses in blue uniforms looking bored, chatting to the barman. There were square wooden tables on a wooden floor, giving it the look of an old-style pub. There were alcoves on the left, down a couple of steps, for those who required a bit of privacy. Each alcove had a film star as its theme, such as Marilyn Monroe, James Dean and Humphrey Bogart. As usual, neither of the waitresses offered to seat them.

'It's always the same,' Chris whispered. 'Let's take one of the alcoves.'

He led Edie to the James Dean alcove and they sat down. One of the waitresses came over, a nice-looking French girl, and handed them each a menu. It was an intimate setting and Chris was willing to bet that more than a few affairs were started in here. Maybe he was about to start one himself.

'It's amazing,' Edie said. 'You'd think they'd advertise or something.'

'Let's hope they don't. I want it to be my secret.'

The waitress came back and Edie ordered a toasted sand-wich and chips. Chris ordered lasagna and diet Cokes for them both.

When she'd disappeared Edie said, 'So are you going to get your pack of cards out?'

Chris smiled. 'I only take them out when I'm on my own. In

fact, this morning was the first time I've ever played on a train. My flat was robbed last night and they took my stereo and TV. I got out the cards for something to do.'

'Sorry to hear that.'

Chris shrugged. 'These things happen. It's not the first time I've been robbed.'

'Well, it must have been fate. If you hadn't been robbed you wouldn't have been playing cards. Then I wouldn't have come over and spoken to you. Have you ever played in a casino?'

Chris nodded. 'A long time ago, on holiday. I played black-jack in Las Vegas and Atlantic City.'

'I've played in Atlantic City as well.'

'I never won anything though.'

Edie laughed. 'I'm not surprised, the way you play.'

Chris felt hurt. 'I told you, I need some coaching.'

'Well, we'll see what we can do.' Edie looked at the pictures on the walls and then back at him. 'You didn't tell me where you work.'

'I run an off-licence called Rowan's, out near Holborn.'

'Is it your own?'

Chris shook his head. 'No. But it's privately owned. My boss had a stroke six months ago though, so I have to run it by myself. Six days a week, which is a bit of a drag.'

'That's tough. What hours do you work?'

'Ten till eight. Sundays, twelve till eight.'

'Can't you get a part-timer?'

'That's what I've suggested, but the owner's a skinflint. If I can run it on my own then why should he waste money? The usual story of all the bosses I've ever worked for. How about you? Have you always been a waitress?'

Edie nodded. 'Just about. I've worked in hotels and pubs as well, though. I get the top wage of three pounds sixty an hour, plus tips.'

'Jesus! That's slave labour.'

'It's not too bad. I can make quite a bit on tips, especially in summer when the Arabs come in. Even more if I leave my top button undone.' She winked.

'I get six pounds an hour,' Chris said.

'That's not too bad.'

'It's not too great either. If I didn't work six days a week, my yearly income would be about fifteen and a half grand. I think I'm worth more than that.'

'Don't we all?' Edie said.

Their meals arrived and, as they ate, Edie told Chris that she'd been at Mario's for nearly a year. Soon she would look for another job though. She found the Trocadero very noisy and claustrophobic. There was always loud music on the PA system and stupid security announcements being made.

'So how old are you?' he asked.

'Twenty-five. How about you?'

Chris wondered whether he should lie but decided against it. Edie seemed pretty sharp to him and she might catch him out.

'Thirty-nine,' he said.

Edie dropped the toasted sandwich she was nibbling and looked at him with wide eyes. 'You're joking!'

Chris shook his head. 'I could lie but what's the point?'

'You look about twenty-nine. What's your secret?'

Chris had been told many times that he looked a lot younger and he didn't really know what his secret was. He supposed it was in his genes. His father had always looked youthful, with hardly any wrinkles on his face even when he was seventy. Chris was the same despite his miserable life. At least that was one good thing he'd inherited.

'I hardly ever go in the sun,' he said, 'and I haven't had a cigarette since my mid-twenties. And I've always had good hair.'

Edie smiled. 'You do have good hair. Hardly any grey at all.'

'And the latest George Clooney cut.'

'That's what I thought when I first saw you! George Clooney. But you look younger than him as well.'

'I think he's about my age, but you're right, I do look

younger. Don't have his money though.' He picked up his Coke for a sip.

For most of his life Chris had let his hair grow fairly long, but it was naturally wavy and thick and always looked a mess. Then, when *ER* had come on TV, he had liked the George Clooney look and had shaved it all off. Now he couldn't bear having it long. For the first time in his life he had straight hair!

'I can safely say,' Edie said, 'that I've never dated a thirty-nine-year-old before.'

'Are we dating?' Chris asked, hopefully.

'Well, we'll see. If you ever meet any of my friends though, you'd better tell them you're twenty-nine!'

Chris laughed.

'And keep your hair short. I like it like that.'

Edie went back to her food and ate her chips with her fingers. 'There's something else you should know about me though, before we go any further.'

Chris waited for the bombshell to drop. She was bisexual. She was a lesbian. She was already married. She had two kids.

Edie looked at him seriously. 'I love to gamble,' she said. 'And I do it a lot.'

Chris nodded. He could live with that. 'Well, you said you played cards in casinos.'

'Any fool can do that. The trick is to do it well.'

'And do you?'

'Yes.'

'Playing blackjack?'

'Yes.'

Chris nodded. He had never met a serious gambler before. Somehow Edie didn't fit the image he had in mind.

She picked up a chip and pointed it at him. 'It just so happens I'm also looking for a partner. And I think you fit the bill.'

Chris blushed. Maybe if he won some money he would be able to afford a new TV and stereo. He put on his best poker face and said, 'You'd better tell me why.'

4

SUNDAY HAD ALWAYS been a day for thinking things through, and that's exactly what Chris did the next day. He sat at the till and looked out of the window at Lambs Conduit Street. It was a pleasant street with some interesting shops, but on Sundays the place just died, except for the locals. The time always dragged, so it was an ideal opportunity, after the papers had been read, to sit and think about the world. Or more specifically, Edie.

He was going to see her tomorrow, his day off, and she'd said she had a little surprise for him. Chris wondered what that surprise would be, his heart beating a little faster at the thought of seeing her again.

Since his only scrape with the law, about six and a half years ago, Chris had been living a very dull and normal life. He had worked in various off-licences and bars, slept with various women without getting too serious, and generally trod a lot of water while awaiting the next momentous event that would teach him something new and give his life the meaning it sorely lacked.

He had spent the tail end of 1991 and the beginning of 1992 waiting for his trial to come around. When it finally arrived in March, he simply took a week off work, then carried on as normal when it was over. He had received a suspended sentence for perverting the course of justice, and continued working in the off-licence in Boroughheath. The case made the local newspaper, but thankfully in only a small write-up without any pictures.

Ron, the manager of the off-licence, never mentioned it to Chris at all, and Chris was pretty sure he never even knew about it. Ron didn't live in the area, so why would he ever pick up a local paper and read it? This had all taught Chris a very valuable lesson: if you kept your mouth shut about things, people very rarely found out. He had ingrained the phrase DON'T TELL ANYONE permanently into his brain, and it had worked remarkably well.

About a month after the trial, Chris handed in his notice and also told the YMCA, where he'd been living at the time, that he would soon be moving on. No one there had heard about his misdeeds either, even his two friends Bill and Ralph. He had been expecting a knock on his door at any moment, asking him to leave the premises, but his DON'T TELL ANYONE plan had obviously been successful there as well.

His girlfriend at the off-licence, seventeen-year-old Rachel, had stuck by him during those difficult months, even though she had caught him two-timing her just before all the shit hit the fan. Chris had been very grateful for her company and support, and when he'd handed in his notice she'd been quite upset. But their relationship had always been doomed, and after several days of talking, he had finally made her realise that fact. She tried persuading him to at least stay in the area, but Chris had always hated Boroughheath and couldn't get out of there quick enough. It was time to move on and make a fresh start.

The day before he left, Chris rang his old girlfriend, Amanda, to say goodbye. Amanda drove round to the YMCA and, much to his surprise, handed back the envelope he'd left with her containing the thousand pounds that he'd illegally obtained from the Boroughheath fiasco. She told him she didn't want his stolen money in her dad's house any more, and wasn't too bothered about ever seeing him again. Chris pecked her on the cheek for goodbye, and watched her walk out of his life.

The next day, he packed all his belongings into two suit-cases and caught a train to Brighton. He had always liked the place on previous visits and he stayed there for three years; working behind bars, keeping a low profile, and enjoying the sea air and atmosphere. He shared a house for a while with a young woman called Jennifer and her three-year old-daughter, Debbie. It was a nice, comfortable, platonic relationship and Chris became extremely fond of Debbie. He started thinking that maybe having a kid would be the way to fill up his empty life, but first he would have to find a suitable woman. A little later, he left Jennifer and Debbie and made his way back to London.

He lived in Finsbury Park for the next year, working in another off-licence, but soon grew uncomfortable with the area and it's general squalor. He visited Elmhurst one day and, on a whim, rented his present room, which was only a couple of hundred yards from the YMCA. He had always liked Elmhurst anyway, and figured that it was better to rent in an area he knew rather than one he didn't. In a way it felt like coming home and surely there would be no ghosts of his past left now.

The door to the off-licence opened and in walked Chris's boss, Rowan. Since his stroke, Rowan had lost about a stone in weight, still had some problems with his speech, and now hobbled along the streets with a walking stick. He was about six foot, with the reddened skin of an alcoholic, and an over-grown ginger beard. He was a scary looking character but had been pretty decent towards Chris, apart from Chris's suggestions about getting a part-timer.

'How's it going?' Rowan asked, closing the front door behind him. He was out of breath, sweating from the short walk from his flat, and looked as if he were about to peg out at any moment.

'Quiet,' Chris said. 'It's the weather. They've probably all left London and headed for the coast.'

'In March? You've got to be kidding.'

'One glimpse of sun is all they need.'

'You may be right.' Rowan looked around at the packed shelves. 'I need a nice bottle of something for lunch. Got some friends coming round.'

Chris doubted that Rowan had any friends at all, and

didn't make any suggestions as to what wine he might like. Rowan would choose what he wanted and then hobble on his weary way home. Chris felt sorry for the guy and often wondered if he would end up the same way. But, over the years, he had managed to get his own drinking under control, and monitored it very closely so it wouldn't get out of hand.

It was a well-known fact that most off-licence managers and pub landlords were or had been alcoholics, and all the off-licences that Chris had worked for had provided counselling for employees with drink problems. His worst time had been back in '91 and '92, just before and after his trial, but since then he had devised a system that he had rigidly stuck to ever since. It was called his 'four-day plan'.

The plan was this: on four days of each week he was not allowed to have any alcohol, while on the other three days he could drink as much as he wanted.

The plan had a two-pronged effect. If he didn't drink for four days each week then there was no way he could become an alcoholic, and if he drank large quantities on the other three days he would feel so rough that he wouldn't want to drink on his dry days. The plan worked perfectly. He also kept a count of drink units in his diary every week, and saw the total falling at the end of every year. He felt that in a year or so he might be able to increase to a 'five-day plan'. It was all a solid back-up against finishing his life in some lonely London gutter.

'I'll take these three,' Rowan said, placing three bottles of red on the counter. Chris wrapped them in brown paper and put them in a carrier bag. 'I need to cash a cheque as well.' Rowan reached into his brown tweed jacket and pulled out a crumpled cheque book.

Chris rang the 'No Sale' button and handed over fifty pounds. He decided to bring up the taboo subject yet again. 'Have you thought any more about getting a part-timer? I've just met a new woman and I could do with some time off.'

Rowan looked at him with envy. 'Oh yeah? When did you meet her?'

'Yesterday. I'm seeing her again tomorrow, and she seems pretty keen.'

'And how old is this one?'

'Twenty-five.'

Rowan laughed. 'You're a case, you are. When are you going to learn?'

'What is there to learn?' Although Chris hadn't been out with anyone for a year, several dates – all in their twenties – had turned up at the shop, all noted by Rowan.

'Don't ask me. I've never been a ladies man. But you're going to have to get hitched some day.'

'Getting hitched is for others,' Chris said.

'Well, I'll think about it. The problem is getting someone we can trust. Do you know anyone?'

'No, but I'll find someone.'

'What do you want. An extra day off?'

'An extra day would be perfect. Like Sundays.'

'And what about keys?'

'I'll get an extra set cut, if that's all right with you.'

Rowan stroked his beard. 'I'll have to check the insurance to make sure we're allowed to give keys to someone else.'

'It should be all right. You don't use yours so there'll still only be two people getting in.'

'I can see you've got it all worked out. I want to hang on to my keys though. Just in case something happens.'

'That's what I reckoned.'

'And we'll need someone very trustworthy. We can't give keys to just anyone.'

Chris sighed. 'I know. I'll use my expert judgement.' He watched the wheels of thought going round in Rowan's head.

'Well, let's put a sign in the window,' Rowan said eventually, 'and see what riff-raff turns up. I don't think I'll be coming back to work for a while and I can't expect you to work six days a week for ever.'

Chris nearly fell off his stool. He couldn't believe what he was hearing. This was a major step forward.

'Good. Thanks, Rowan.'

Rowan nodded, picked up his carrier, muttered 'See you anon,' and walked out of the door.

Chris almost felt like having a drink to celebrate but stopped himself. After all, Sunday was his last non-drinking day of the current week.

5

THEY HAD ARRANGED to meet the next day at Charing Cross station. Chris was a few minutes early so he stood next to WH Smith and watched all the people streaming in from the suburbs and the coast. Soon it would be the tourist season and it could only get worse; already there were groups of French schoolchildren sitting on the concourse with their rucksacks.

Edie had told him that she lived in Orpington, just a few stops down the line from Elmhurst. Apart from that, all Chris knew for sure from their first date was that she wanted a playing partner so she could win bigger amounts at the blackjack table. Apparently, she played two or three times a week after work and won regularly because she was a card counter. But if you played in a team you could win more.

Chris knew that card counting was the only way you could win regularly at blackjack but it was something he had never tried. On the few occasions he'd played in the past he had more or less stuck to what they called Basic Strategy, which was a system worked out over the years by professionals, where you ended up playing the percentages. You could never win large amounts playing Basic Strategy unless you had a lucky run of cards. It was just a system whereby you broke even, won small amounts, or didn't lose too much.

Chris thought back to the two times he had played black-jack in casinos. Both had been on holidays in America when he'd been in his twenties; the first in Atlantic City, the second in Las Vegas. Both trips had been with his old girlfriend, Kristina, and while she had been getting hooked on slot machines, he had been getting hooked on blackjack. He had bought a simple book that included the Basic Strategy tables, and tried learning it quickly in his hotel room. He had then gone to the tables and played for lengthy spells without losing too much. He had forgotten most of the strategy since, but it looked like he would soon be re-learning it with Edie.

A few minutes later he saw her. She was walking up platform five wearing a smart black skirt, blue blouse, and brown suede jacket. She looked anything but a waitress now. She had phoned him at work yesterday evening and asked him not to wear jeans. She'd said she had a surprise for him and that he was to wear smart trousers and a shirt. Chris hated wearing smart trousers but did as he was told. He had dug out an old black pair, a blue-and-white striped shirt, and a dark blue sports jacket. The last time he had worn the trousers had been to someone's funeral over five years ago. He hoped it wasn't an omen.

Edie greeted him with a big smile and they complimented each other on their outfits. Chris suggested they go to one of the boat pubs on the Thames and Edie thought that was a great idea. It was a warm day, far too warm for March.

They walked down to the Embankment, along the Thames for a few minutes, then over a walkway on to one of the boats. They bought drinks at the deck bar then sat down at a table. Edie produced a pack of cards, a box of matches, and some larger cards with rows of numbers on them. They were the only people there.

'Do you know what these are?' Edie asked, pointing to the numbered cards.

Chris nodded. 'They look like Basic Strategy tables.'

Edie smiled. 'Very good. The basic rules that every player should learn before he even goes near a blackjack table.'

'I tried learning them once before but never did it properly. You'd better start from scratch.'

'That's why most people lose. They never learn a thing before they start playing. Ninety-five per cent of people who walk into casinos don't know what they're doing.'

Chris nodded and glanced out over the water. A tourist boat went past and a few people waved at him. He ignored them.

'The blackjack player who plays without much knowledge,' Edie continued, 'who just plays on hunches, starts off with a three to five per cent disadvantage over the casinos. If you learn the Basic Strategy, you cut that disadvantage to between point five and one per cent.'

'That doesn't sound too promising,' Chris said.

'It isn't, but it's the minimum that all serious players should have. Gambling mathematicians have worked it out over the years. In fact, the first man to do it was called Edward Thorp. He wrote a revolutionary book called *Beat The Dealer* in the '60s which contained the first Basic Strategy tables. It became a bestseller and casinos had to change their rules because too many people started winning. Any serious book on blackjack will have these tables in it. They're common knowledge to all regular players.'

'Okay,' Chris said. He was already amazed at how much Edie knew. She was also very businesslike in the way she explained things. He wondered if he liked what he was seeing. He picked up his pint for a sip.

'It shouldn't be too hard for you to re-learn,' Edie said, 'as you've already tried in the past. This evening I'll take you to a casino and let you try it out.'

Chris nearly choked on his beer. 'We're going to a casino this evening?'

'If you've no objections.'

Chris couldn't think of any except for the fact that he didn't want to lose any money. 'No, not really. I just didn't bring that much money with me.'

'We could go to a cash machine.'

'How much will I need?'

'Fifty pounds should be enough.'

'And this is fifty pounds I'm going to lose?'

'Maybe. But if you learn these tables before we go, you may well win.'

'How about you. Are you going to win?'

'I usually do.'

Chris fell silent. Did he really want to go to a casino and

lose fifty pounds? Now he knew why Edie had asked him to wear smart clothes.

'So how can you afford to gamble,' he asked, 'when you're working for the minimum wage?'

'I told you, I get good tips as well. All my small change adds up. Plus I have a stake.'

'A stake?'

'Yes. I've saved up over the years. All good gamblers have a stake. They only bet what they can afford to lose. I have a minimum stake of a thousand pounds. I try not to go below that. At the moment I'm working my way up from there. I've actually got over fifteen hundred at the moment.'

'That's fifteen hundred more than I've got.' Chris thought he'd better keep quiet about the thousand he had stashed away. He didn't want to be gambling that.

'The sensible gambler just plays for short periods regularly,' Edie said. 'That's what I do. I pop in after work and sometimes I'm only in there for twenty minutes. If I get ahead I get out. One time I went in, I won eighty pounds on the first hand. I took the money and walked straight back out again.'

'I think I would too.'

'The bad gambler will stay there for long periods. He'll think it's his lucky night, and maybe for a while it will be. But the longer you play the more chance you have of losing. The odds of the casino will always grind you down in the end.'

'It doesn't sound like much fun.'

'It isn't most of the time. I look at it as a business. It's a way to supplement my income. But of course, I don't just stick to Basic Strategy. As I told you on Saturday, I'm also a card counter.'

Chris was starting to look at Edie in a totally different light, a good-looking waitress card shark who was about to take him under her wing. He told himself not to underestimate her. He had made that mistake before and got into trouble for it. What exactly was he getting mixed up in? Was Edie interested in him or just using him as part of her larger game plan? He would have to make an instant decision on this one, and get out quick if things looked a little dodgy.

'I've heard of card counting,' he said. 'But I don't know exactly what it is.'

Edie picked up a crisp from an open bag they were sharing on the table. She nibbled at it as she talked. 'Card counting is keeping track of the cards as they're being dealt so that you more or less know when some good cards are going to be coming your way, i.e. some tens or aces. When the odds are in your favour you up your bets and hopefully collect on some good hands. It's the only way you can make serious money at blackjack. You'll never make it with just the Basic Strategy.'

'So you really have to learn two systems to get ahead?'

'At least. There are lots of variations on card counting though. People have their own different systems, and also different betting systems. But we can go into that later.'

Chris scratched his head. 'Yeah, I'd prefer one step at a time.'

'Okay.' Edie picked up the cards. 'Let's teach you the Basic Strategy.'

They played for thirty minutes at the table, but then a barman came over and told them they'd have to move on. He didn't want people playing cards. Office workers were now drifting in for lunchtime drinks and they were obviously taking up valuable space. Edie started to argue with him but Chris gave her a soft kick under the table and she calmed down. He didn't like playing with other people around anyway.

They left the boat and found a small park near Embankment tube and sat on a vacant bench. More office workers were sprawled on the lawns, eating sandwiches and drinking soft drinks. One hint of sun and people appeared from nowhere.

They sat apart on the bench, Edie laying a newspaper between them. She put the Basic Strategy tables in front of

Chris so he could see them as he played, and then started dealing. They had twenty matches each again, each match repre-
senting five pounds – the minimum bet at the casino they'd be
going to later. Chris thought five pounds was far too high. If he
had ten bad hands he'd be off the table in no time.

They started off slowly, Chris checking the tables with
nearly every hand to make sure he was making the right move.
Edie was patient and talked him through, explaining why some
moves were mathematically sound and others weren't. For
instance, in the past, if he'd been dealt twelve after two cards he
would always have asked for another (or draw as Edie called
it). But now he realised that if the dealer's up card was a four,
five, or six he should stick (or stand) on the twelve, because the
dealer had a good chance of busting. This was because dealers
always had to draw if their totals were sixteen or under and,
sure enough, it seemed to work more often than not.

Once this rule was ingrained in his head, Chris learnt all
about splitting pairs, then doubling down, then hard and soft
totals when he was dealt an ace. He had never thought a
simple game of pontoon, as he'd always called it when he was
a child, could be so difficult.

It was fun playing with Edie too. She obviously took great
pleasure in winning his matches and she laughed at his fum-
bling and mistakes. He wondered what she'd be like in a casino.

After a couple of hours Chris had had enough. Most of the
office workers had disappeared and there was a chill coming
into the air. He put his cards down and stretched. 'Can we
have a break?' he asked.

'Sure. You seem to be getting the hang of it.'

'I think I'm confident enough to play tonight.'

'We can play sooner than that if you like. The casinos open
at two.'

Chris looked at his watch. It was nearly four o'clock. 'Let's
go and get some tea first.'

'Okay. I know a place,' Edie said. 'But would you like to go
to a cash machine first?'

6

THE CASINO THEY were visiting was called The Golden Fleece on Shaftesbury Avenue. Chris could feel himself getting nervous as they approached it.

'Are you a member here?' he asked.

'You always have to be a member,' Edie said. 'You can't just walk in off the streets and play.'

'You can in Vegas.'

'It's different over here. You have to apply twenty-four hours in advance in every London casino.'

'Sounds like a lot of hassle.'

'It keeps the idiots out. Think what it would be like if they let football supporters in on Saturday nights without asking questions.'

Chris nodded. 'Point taken.'

The entrance to the casino was quite small. Chris had walked down Shaftesbury Avenue many times in his life and had never noticed it.

They pushed open the doors and were greeted at reception by two men. One of them smiled at Edie. She signed her name on a card and Chris had to do the same. They left their coats with a cloakroom lady then started climbing some stairs to the left. There were paintings of horses on the walls.

'You're well known here then,' Chris said.

'Only at the front desk fortunately. I don't want to be well known on the casino floor.'

'Why not?'

'Because it's bad to be conspicuous. A card counter should always be as anonymous as possible. Fortunately, I'm also a woman. In the chauvinistic casino world, women are seen as bad gamblers and no-hopers. That means I can count cards and no one really looks at me.'

'Is card counting frowned upon then?'

'Of course. If you're caught, you're thrown out and banned from every casino in London. Card counting is viewed as cheating. They don't like it one little bit.'

'Jesus. You didn't tell me that before.'

'Well, we haven't got on to card counting yet.'

'Will they throw me out for using Basic Strategy?'

Edie laughed. 'No. They only throw you out if you start winning.'

They reached the top of the stairs and walked into the casino. Chris was surprised and disappointed at how small it was. The casinos in Atlantic City and Vegas had been as big as football pitches, but this one was about as big as a penalty area.

'It's minute,' he said.

'Size doesn't matter,' Edie said. 'All you need is one table and a dealer.'

There was a bar/restaurant on the right where people sat eating burgers and chips. There was a sign saying you could get a meal for £1. Most of the gamblers seemed to be foreign, either Arabic or Oriental, and it was very smoky.

'Spot the Englishman,' Chris said.

'I know,' Edie said. 'Maybe English people don't have any money these days. Remember we're right next to Chinatown though. That's where all the Chinese come from. I'm always amazed at how much money they throw away. Especially the women on roulette.'

'Maybe it's drug money,' Chris whispered.

Edie looked at him. 'I hadn't thought of that.'

'I've got a suspicious mind.'

As they walked around the room they passed roulette and blackjack tables, then some punto banco. Each roulette table had an electronic scoreboard, showing the last twenty or so numbers that had won. Chris found it interesting to see if there were any sequences coming up on the tables. He found himself staring at the women croupiers as well, who wore long purple dresses and looked like grounded flight attendants. He watched them scraping up the chips and spinning the wheels and wondered why they would want to work in such an unhealthy, monotonous atmosphere. He had found working in smoky pubs unbearable after a while, but at least he could talk to the punters and have a laugh. There didn't seem to be much fun going on in here. Everyone looked so serious. He pointed it out to Edie.

'The croupiers have to be serious,' she said. 'There's a lot of money going around. They also have to keep an eye out for cheats.'

'People cheat at roulette?'

'There are lots of ways. They work in teams. For example, distract the croupier and put your money down after the ball has dropped.'

'You're joking! And they get away with it?'

'Apparently. The good con artists are like magicians. You don't know you've been had until afterwards.'

After going round the room once, Edie pointed to the blackjack table she wanted. 'It's usually best to play on a quiet table. The percentages rise slightly if there are fewer people playing. Also, if you're counting you don't want any distractions. You can sit to my left.'

They approached a table. There was only one player, sitting to the right. Edie left two seats vacant next to him and took the middle one. Chris took the one on Edie's left. He watched her take two fifty-pound notes out of her handbag and give them to the dealer.

'One hundred pounds,' said the dealer, and then pushed over some chips.

Chris took his money out of his pocket and handed it over.

'Fifty pounds,' said the dealer, and then Chris had ten five-pound chips sitting in front of him. Edie smiled reassuringly.

'Place your bets,' said the dealer.

Chris felt some butterflies in his stomach and saw the man

on the right put some chips down. Edie put a five-pound chip in front of her and Chris did the same. Then the cards started flashing across the table.

The first hand was easy. Chris got a king and a ten, and the dealer bust. He was five pounds ahead already. He smiled at Edie but she didn't look at him; she was concentrating on the cards as they left the dealers hand. Chris tried to remember what she'd told him about shutting out all other distractions so he fixed his eyes on the dealer, a young man in his twenties, dressed in a crimson waistcoat with a black bow tie. Then he focused on the cards and nothing else. It didn't do much good.

He lost the next five hands, even though he reckoned he played them correctly. Then he won a couple of hands but lost another five after that. All of a sudden he only had three chips in front of him. He was then dealt a pair of eights and couldn't remember whether he should split them or not. He felt sweat breaking out on his forehead. He looked at Edie but she was too focused on her cards. He decided to take a hit and he bust. Now he only had two chips left.

Two hands later and it was all over. He stood up, feeling like an incompetent, and Edie said quietly, 'See you in the bar.'

Chris did as he was told, walked over to the small bar and bought himself a beer. He sat at a table brooding about his loss, fifty pounds in about ten minutes. There must be better ways of having fun.

Edie joined him about half an hour later.

'How did you do?' he asked.

'Twenty pounds up,' Edie said, sitting down next to him.

'Is it really worth it?'

'You have to be patient. Sometimes I win a lot more than that. But if you think about it, that's twenty pounds in under an hour. That's a whole lot more than three pounds sixty an hour. That's the way I look at it.'

'But you couldn't do it for eight hours a day.'

'No. You'd be mad to want to. But as I told you before, I just do it to supplement my income. Anyway, as I told you on

Saturday, I'm looking for a partner. I think I can make bigger money that way.'

'Tell me more.'

'Let's go somewhere else.'

They went downstairs, picked up their coats, and left the casino. They headed back up Shaftesbury Avenue, crossed the road, and walked into Soho. They found a pub that wasn't too crowded and sat at a table with their drinks.

'I've been reading a book about a character called Ken Uston,' Edie said. 'He's widely regarded as the best blackjack player ever.'

Chris shook his head. 'I've never heard of him.'

'You wouldn't have unless you know about blackjack. Uston was a senior vice president of the Pacific Stock Exchange who packed it all in to play blackjack professionally in the '70s and '80s. He was highly intelligent, a master of disguise, and a well-known nuisance to casinos all over America. He used to get barred all the time. He was famous for organising teams of card counters who would hit the casinos and take them for a ride.'

'How did that work?'

'He would place card counters, say one at each of five different tables, and when the cards on that table were favourable, the card counter would signal one of his accomplices who would be walking around the casino looking like a casual gambler or a drunk. The punter would come over to the table, start laying big bets like a high roller, and hopefully collect some large winnings thanks to the card counter. The card counter would just keep playing normally, giving signals about size of bets and when to play, and keeping a low profile. The high roller would collect and then disappear. Later they would divide the money between them.'

'Sounds like good fun.'

'It is if it works. It would have to be very well worked out.'

'And this is what you want me to get involved in?'

'I thought it might be fun to give it a go. On a much smaller scale though.'

Chris was starting to feel worried, although he had to admit the idea did sound intriguing. He didn't know if he could act like a high-rolling drunk though.

'How much do you think we could win?' he asked.

'I don't know. If we can do it for a few months, two or three times a week, the sky's the limit.'

Chris thought about it. 'What about our jobs? We both work long hours.'

'Casinos are open until two in the morning. We'd have plenty of time. Last trains home are at midnight. You don't start work until ten do you?'

'No. If I stay sober the lack of sleep won't matter much.'

'We'll be staying sober all right. Drinking is one thing we won't be doing.'

Chris thought about his savings. He hadn't added to his thousand pounds, the thousand pounds Amanda had given him, for about six months. It would be nice if he could double or treble it. Plus, he still had over eight hundred pounds on his Visa to pay off for the hi-fi equipment that was no longer in his room.

'Did Ken Uston ever get caught with his teams?' he asked.

'Lots of times. He got beaten up more than once as well.'

'I could do without any of that.'

'I wouldn't put us in any danger.'

'I'm glad to hear it.'

They fell silent for a minute. Chris looked at the evening crowd surrounding them. The bar was full of smoke and loud talking. It seemed his life had never followed the uncomplicated route, and now it looked as though it was about to take another deviation.

'Will I have to learn to card count?' he asked.

'No. I'll do all that. But you'll have to improve your Basic Strategy.'

'Yeah. I felt inadequate tonight.'

'It doesn't matter. You're only starting out. Here, you can take this home with you.' Edie took a small book out of her handbag and gave it to him. It was called *The Basics Of Winning Blackjack*. 'Read that from cover to cover, memorise your tables, and we'll have another go next week.'

'Okay.' Chris took the book and slipped it into his jacket pocket. 'And what happened to Ken Uston? Is he still making money from blackjack?'

Edie shook her head. 'No. He was found dead in a Paris hotel room at the age of fifty-two.'

Chris smiled. He should've known it didn't have a happy ending.

7

CHRIS DIDN'T SLEEP very well that night. He dreamt he was Ken Uston, staying in a Paris hotel room, drinking champagne with a busty blonde after some big winnings in a casino. Then he was lying on the bed, his arms behind his head, as the blonde went down on him. When he was about to come he woke up, which always happened with sex dreams.

He lay awake for two hours thinking about it. Edie had told him that when Ken Uston had been found dead he, too, had been lying with his arms behind his head, a satisfied smile on his face. Chris found the image worrying, although he supposed it signified that Uston died happy. Or maybe he'd just drunk a little too much champagne, as Uston was prone to do. Chris drifted back to sleep around five o'clock, then the alarm woke him up at seven-thirty.

He climbed slowly out of bed and drew the curtains. His room overlooked the quiet end of Elmhurst High Street, although the tree growing from the pavement obscured about half of the view. Directly opposite, on the other side of the road, was a pond where people walked their dogs and pushed their prams. Half a dozen ducks floated around, making a serene suburban scene.

The wood around the windows was old and rotten and, in the winter, Chris plugged the gaps with Plasticine to keep out the draft. He looked at the bits of red, green and blue, and supposed that in a month or so he could start peeling them out. That would be something to look forward to.

He had all his belongings in this one room and it was slightly larger than the one he used to have in the YMCA. The house had been built at the beginning of the century, and he had painted the walls pale pink when he'd moved in. The wall by his bed sloped towards the ceiling and had bad condensation in the winter. Large pieces of paint were flaking off, and when he had the heating on, the wall would sweat and drip, leaving long vertical stains.

There was no central heating in the house so all the lodgers had portable gas fires. When the gas bottle ran out, Chris had to wheel it down the road on an old shopping trolley to get a refill from a hardware shop; one of the most demeaning tasks he had ever had to endure in all his renting days. There was a strict rule against anyone using electric fires, as the landlord paid all the electrical bills, and it was written into each lease that if any were found on the premises, they would be confiscated. Chris, however, had a fan heater stored in his wardrobe for emergencies. If the gas bottle ran out during weekends, for instance, there was no way he was going to freeze for a few days until he could get to the hardware shop on the Monday. The landlord obviously hadn't thought about that little problem when writing his detailed rules and regulations.

Chris grabbed a towel and walked on to the landing. He walked past the small empty room on his right, then down the couple of steps past John's room. On the floor below there was another small room that was empty, right next to Heavy Metal's room. Chris had stayed there for a few months when he'd first moved in, before moving upstairs. His neighbour had been a recently divorced man in his forties, who'd played loud disco music and had flashing lights rigged up. He brought divorced women back to his den, so Chris had to put up with vigorous lovemaking as well as the disco beat. It had been a very trying time, and he had dreaded going home every night. He had been certain a little S & M had been going on in there as well and had been relieved when his present room became vacant. Soon after, the disco freak moved out as well, to be replaced by Heavy Metal.

When all the rooms were full the house held five lodgers, and they had to share one bathroom and the kitchen. There were four of them there at present because of Heavy Metal's girlfriend, who was illegally sharing. It was one of the worst places Chris had ever lived but he had got so used to living badly in rented rooms that he hardly gave it a second thought these days, as long as the rent was cheap. The single life never ran smoothly, always attracting the flotsam of life, and he'd never be free of it until he had his own place. But he couldn't see that happening for quite a while.

When he reached the bathroom he tried the door but it was locked. He could hear splashing sounds so someone was in the bath. He swore under his breath. He never had a bath in the morning because he knew everyone would be trying to get into the bathroom. He thought it was a selfish thing to do and wished it was a general rule. He went back to his room where he kept a plastic bucket for emergencies.

He turned on the kettle and waited while it boiled. When it was ready, he poured some hot water into the bucket, which already had several inches of cold in it. He stripped off and washed himself with a flannel, trying not to think about his bursting bladder. He cleaned his crotch and under his arms, put on talc and deodorant, and then got quickly dressed. He went back downstairs to the bathroom but it was still engaged. He swore again and went back to his room.

For urine emergencies, he kept an empty plastic litre bottle of Britvic orange juice in his wardrobe, but tried to use it only during the night if he woke up. He would then empty the bottle down the toilet, rinsing it with hot water. He liked the Britvic bottle because it had a wide opening and a snap on top. He reached for it now and relieved himself.

Feeling better, he slotted two pieces of bread into his toaster, and made himself a cup of tea. He would usually watch *The Big Breakfast* while eating, but as he now had no TV he just sat and stared out of the window. He watched kids making their way to school, and cars starting to clog up the road.

After cleaning his teeth and spitting into the bucket, he picked up his jacket and headed downstairs. As he passed the bathroom he saw that it was now vacant.

*

As he made his way to the station, Chris once again couldn't get Edie out of his mind, but just where he stood with her at the moment he really didn't know.

After their drinks in the pub last night, he had taken her to Pizza Express in Soho. She'd drunk mineral water and talked most of the time about blackjack. She was obviously obsessed with the game and determined to prove herself at it. When he tried asking some personal questions, she just moved the subject back to gambling. All he had found out was that she didn't like working in London, and that someday she would like to settle in the country but still carry on gambling. When he suggested there wouldn't be many casinos in the country, she told him she'd find one in a nearby town. There were more around than people knew and she could prove it; she had a world guide to casinos at home that listed just about every one in existence. Chris didn't doubt it for a minute.

When he got to work, Chris stuck a notice in the window saying 'Sunday worker needed. 12-8. Experience preferable.' If he offered them five pounds an hour then Rowan would be saving a pound an hour. Surely he would be satisfied with that.

He opened the door and started refilling the shelves. He was looking forward to the end of the day already. He would visit Virgin Megastore afterwards and buy a blackjack computer disk. Edie had told him last night that she used one at home to keep on top of her game. Chris had decided he would try and impress her when they made their next assault on the casinos. Apparently, you could buy a disc that taught you not only Basic Strategy, but also how to card count. He would retrieve his neglected laptop computer from the bottom of his wardrobe and put it to some creative use at last.

8

A TRIP TO Sainsbury's on Thursdays for late-night food shopping wasn't a weekly outing that Dave Brill looked forward to. It was always too crowded and he felt like an idiot wheeling the trolley behind Evelyn, his overweight wife. He also wanted to hide when his two kids, Tony and Joanna, started pulling sweets and soft drinks off the racks, then insisted on going no further until they were deposited in the trolley. It was enough to drive a man to drink or violence, or question his role in modern-day life. And it was enough to make a man pray that his mobile phone would ring so he could wander down an aisle and get away for a few minutes. And, as if in answer to his prayers, Dave Brill's mobile rang at that precise moment.

The tune Brill had picked for his mobile was 'Land Of Hope And Glory.' He was a patriotic man and liked listening to the tune before turning it off. He also thought that other people should listen to it as well, so he would deliberately take his time unclipping the mobile from his waist and bringing it to his ear, actions that drove Evelyn to despair whenever she was around.

'Hello?' said Brill. He signaled to Evelyn to carry on without him, then wandered away by himself.

He talked for about five minutes to one of his builder friends about the possibility of a chimney job and then hung up. The call had been too short for his liking and he decided to wander around some more. Then he saw a face he recognised in one of the other aisles, next to a display of discounted cakes.

He was a man in his mid-thirties with short brown hair, good-looking in an ordinary kind of way. He was walking around with a wire basket, putting food in quickly like he knew exactly what he wanted, and spending the shortest amount of time possible in front of the shelves. Brill watched and envied him; the single man collecting single meals, no family worries to contend with.

'Gone on strike?'

Brill jumped at the voice. Evelyn was standing right behind him, and Tony and Joanna were looking up at him with chocolate-smeared faces.

Brill forced a smile. 'No. I just saw someone I recognised. See that bloke over there in the leather jacket? The one with the short hair?'

Evelyn looked where he was pointing. 'He looks like George Clooney.'

Brill felt a pang of jealousy. He didn't fancy his wife any more, except when he was feeling horny, but he still didn't like her fancying other men. 'I've seen him somewhere but I can't figure out where. Do you recognise him?'

Evelyn shook her head. 'Why don't you go and ask him?'

'You be all right without me?'

'Well, you're not exactly helping at the moment.' She grabbed the trolley and nudged him out of the way.

Brill watched his family disappear, then walked down an aisle and started circling round his quarry. He was still racking his brain, thinking maybe he'd been to school with the bloke, or maybe played in the same football team when they were in their twenties, or maybe they just drank in the same pub. He decided to approach the man and ask him outright, but when he was about five feet away he remembered, and had to veer sharply away.

His heart beat a little faster as he walked towards a video display rack. He picked up a copy of *The Lion King* and turned to look again. It was him all right, even though he had shorter hair than the last time he'd seen him. He had seen him in the flesh only once before but he'd always been good at remembering faces. Names were a different matter.

He watched as the man headed for the checkout and then

went to find Evelyn. She was stuck in a long queue with a massive trolley load of food. Brill always wondered how they ate so much. 'Are you all right here?' he asked.

'Did you find out who he was?'

'I'm just going outside for a minute. I want to have a chat with him. I'll see you back at the car.'

'Well, don't be too long. There's a lot of frozen food in here.'

Brill left by the front exit and leant on the railings outside. Then he started to sweat because maybe the man had a car and would leave by the car park exit at the rear. But a few minutes later he saw him walking towards him carrying two bags, and he let out a relieved sigh.

He turned his back and looked at Elmhurst High Street, and when he sensed the man was near he looked right and left over his shoulders to see which way he was going. He saw him going to the right and followed.

Elmhurst High Street hardly deserved the name because, apart from Sainsbury's, there were no other shops of interest unless you were a local. Brill walked past an electrical shop, a shoe shop, a Chinese restaurant, two estate agents and a video shop. They were heading towards Elmhurst pond, and then the man turned right, next to a pub called The Pilgrim's Rest. Brill jogged to catch up and then saw him disappearing through a gate on the other side of the road. He waited a few moments, walked up to the gate and looked through it.

On the left stood a couple of dustbins, and in front of him, some stone steps leading up towards a green door on the first floor. Brill walked up and found three buzzers with names next to them. They said Humphrey, Epstein and Small. Brill knew which one it was straight away. He snarled and went back down the steps.

He found his wife and kids waiting in the car at Sainsbury's. The kids were in the back seat eating ice-creams. They ate them all year round.

'About time,' Evelyn said as he climbed in. 'Curiosity satisfied?'

'More than satisfied,' Brill said.

'So who is he?'

Brill saw the keys sitting in the ignition and turned them. He fastened his seat-belt and said, 'He was no one. I got him mixed up with someone else.'

His wife gave him a funny look and went back to the magazine she was reading. Brill put the car into first gear.

On Friday morning, a young man came into the off-licence and asked Chris about the vacancy in the window. He said his name was Hugh Blake and he was twenty-four. He was dressed neatly in grey trousers and light-blue shirt, and his dark hair was swept back over his forehead, Elvis style. He was polite and articulate, showed enthusiasm and even smiled, four qualities that had been missing in the people Chris had seen so far.

'Have you ever worked in an off-licence before?' he asked him.

Hugh shook his head. 'No. But I worked in Hamleys once. The one in Covent Garden. I know how to work tills.'

'Well that's the main thing,' Chris said. 'How long were you there?'

'Six months or so,' Hugh said. 'Then I went abroad.'

They chatted a while and Chris showed him round the shop and told him what the job would entail. It turned out that Hugh was really an English teacher, teaching English as a foreign language. He had just come back from a lengthy spell in Greece, and would be on his way to Estonia, of all places, for more of the same. He had about six months to kill and wanted part-time jobs to tide him over. Sunday work was fine with him, and if he could get any extra then that would be no problem either. He seemed like the perfect candidate so Chris asked him to come back on Sunday, when he could show him the ropes. They shook hands and he left.

Just before closing time, Rowan came in to pick up some weekend booze. His face looked even redder than usual and

Chris wondered if he was drinking himself to death. He watched as he hobbled round with his walking stick, looking at the shelves. He was getting thinner by the week and looked like a walking skeleton.

'I've found someone to work on Sundays,' he told Rowan, as he wrapped up his bottles.

Rowan looked surprised. 'That was quick. Is she young and good-looking?'

'She's a man,' Chris said. 'He's an English teacher killing time between jobs. Seems like a nice bloke.'

'Trustworthy?'

'Seemed honest enough.'

'That's the main thing. Any references?'

'I didn't bother asking. References are pretty meaningless anyway. When was the last time you saw a bad reference?'

'Did you ever give me any?'

'No. And you trust me, don't you?'

'Like you were my own,' Rowan smiled. 'How much are you paying him?'

'Five pounds an hour. You'll be saving money.'

'Well, I can't be bothered with the extra paperwork. Can you pay him yourself and keep the difference?'

'Are you sure?'

'It's easier that way. That means you'll be getting a pound an hour for doing nothing. Can't say fairer than that.'

'Thanks, Rowan. Sounds like a good deal to me.'

Rowan wandered off and Chris sat at the till, feeling pleased with himself. Not only would he soon be getting Sundays off, he would be getting paid a little for them as well! Things were looking up all the time.

9

FOR HIS THIRD meeting with Edie, Chris was once again dressed smartly. He was meeting her at the Shaftesbury Avenue entrance to the Trocadero and she was there waiting for him on Monday afternoon, wearing a white blouse, thin black leather jacket, grey slacks and black leather boots. He gave her a kiss on the cheek but there was no reaction at all, she might even have flinched. He wondered if this relationship was ever going to go anywhere.

'Today we're going to two casinos,' she said. 'The first one's called Lester's.'

'Okay.'

'It's just over the road.'

They crossed to the other side and took the first turning on the left, down Archer Street. It was narrow and deserted, and Chris was glad it was still daylight. On the right there was a dilapidated sign, going down the wall, saying C A S I N O with large neon playing cards next to it. They entered through a door into a tiny reception, where two men awaited them. Once again, Edie took out her membership card, handed it over, and they both signed a form.

They left their coats and pushed through some swing doors, straight into the casino. This one was even smaller than The Golden Fleece; a rectangular room about the size of your average café. There were blackjack tables down the left and some roulette tables at the back. The walls had a fake stone look to them, making it seem as if they were in a cave. Chris noticed black spheres attached to the ceiling over every table, which he presumed were cameras.

'The eye in the sky,' Edie said. 'Big Brother is watching you.'

'Great,' Chris said. 'That really makes me feel at ease.'

'Just ignore them.'

She led him down a staircase to some more tables, including one for craps, where three young croupiers sat with bored expressions waiting for punters to turn up. Edie disappeared to the ladies, so Chris asked the three croupiers to explain the rules to him. He stood there with glazed eyes and nodded, and didn't understand a word of what they told him. He was glad when Edie returned.

Back upstairs, they sat at a blackjack table and Chris bought fifty pounds' worth of chips, while Edie once again had a hundred pounds. Playing five pounds each hand, and sticking to Basic Strategy, he soon found that he was twenty-five pounds ahead. Edie said quietly to him, 'I would quit if I were you.'

Chris looked at her with surprise but saw she was serious.

'There's a bar upstairs,' she said. 'Wait for me there.'

Feeling a little embarrassed, Chris picked up his chips and cashed them at a window at the back, that had vertical bars like some kind of Wild West bank. Then he walked back past Edie – she didn't even glance at him – out through the doors, and upstairs.

The bar was small, with a tiny restaurant attached. He bought a bottle of Beck's and the barman opened a complimentary packet of crisps into a dish in front of him. Chris almost started laughing. Was this high-roller treatment?

Despite his quick departure from the table, Chris was feeling quite pleased with himself. He had practised quite a lot on his computer with his new Masque Blackjack game, and the extra bit of knowledge seemed to have paid off. He looked at the menu and saw that a three-course meal would only cost him six pounds ninety five. There were two old ladies chattering away at one of the tables.

'Quiet tonight?' he asked the barman. He was a short man in his forties, with a large mole on his right cheek.

'It gets busier later,' the man said. He was filling in a book full of figures.

Chris didn't know what else to say. His ability at small talk had been deserting him recently. He could talk to customers in the shop about wine, but once he was out of that environment he tended to struggle.

'I'm quitting soon anyway,' the barman said.

'Why's that?' Chris asked.

'I'm learning The Knowledge. I'm going to become a taxi driver in a few months.'

'That's good,' Chris said, and then learnt a few facts about taxi driving that he'd never known before. Once the man had learnt his Knowledge, he would buy a cab for £26,000. He would then be his own boss and work what hours he wanted, although he reckoned he'd still have to work eight to ten hours a day to keep his family. He said there were over 20,000 black cabs in London.

Chris found it all quite interesting and it was nice to have a conversation with someone, even if that other person was doing most of the talking. It almost made him feel human again. He supposed he was learning his own kind of Knowledge with Edie and he wondered where she was. He looked at his watch and saw that half an hour had passed.

The barman went back to his paperwork without asking Chris anything about himself. Chris's experience over the years was that most people were only interested in themselves, and they only asked things about you so they could ultimately bring the conversation back to themselves. Chris thought Edie was a prime example. Miss One-Track Blackjack Mind.

It was another fifteen minutes before she appeared and she didn't look too happy.

'Five pounds,' she said. 'Five pounds won in an hour's play. It's obviously not going to happen here tonight.'

'At least you didn't lose,' Chris said.

She gave him a dirty look and said, 'Let's go.'

Chris waved goodbye to the barman and wished him good luck with his Knowledge.

*

The next casino was called Bonaparte's and it was in Leicester Square. They stepped off the street and headed down some stairs.

After leaving their coats at reception, they walked down some more stairs to a landing, where a large aquarium sat. Chris stopped to look at the fish but Edie just carried on walking.

He found her in the bar, sitting on a comfortable sofa sipping a lemonade. There was a bottle of Beck's sitting on the table for him.

He sat down next to her and almost disappeared into the softness. She was watching a TV, high on the wall, showing an old football match. She didn't speak for about five minutes.

'You like football?' he asked to break the silence.

'Not much. How about you?'

'I've supported Crystal Palace all my life. But they're not doing too well at the moment. Sometimes I go and watch them.'

He looked at Edie and she just nodded. 'I feel more relaxed now,' she said. 'Shall we go and give it another go?'

'What about my beer?'

She looked at his bottle as if it were an intruder. 'You can't take that in there. You finish it and then join me.'

Chris watched her stand up and disappear through a doorway.

He sat looking at the TV screen. It was a match from four years ago and he wondered why it was on. Did they just play old football videos? Who on earth would be interested?

Edie was getting on his nerves tonight but he would let it slide for now. After all, he didn't have anything else going on in his life so he may as well stick with her. And she was still very fanciable. He wondered if she'd be this distant in bed. He thought back to one of his old flings, a girl he'd once worked with who had always struck him as being very aloof. One evening, drunk on vodka, she had asked him to go to bed with her and, much to his surprise, she had turned out to be very passionate. It had been a very erotic evening, but when Chris had asked for a repeat she had declined, reverting to her aloof ways. Maybe Edie would be the same pleasant surprise. It was something worth thinking about.

He finished his beer and walked into the casino. The smoke hit him in waves as soon as he entered. It was slightly bigger than Lester's but still very small. He spotted Edie on the other side of the room.

All the seats were taken at her table so he stood behind and watched. There were other people watching as well. About five minutes later a seat became available, the first seat on the dealer's left. Chris jumped into it and handed over sixty pounds. He looked across at Edie. There were two people sitting between them and plenty of others milling around behind.

He played his Basic Strategy for twenty minutes without really getting anywhere. He won a little, lost a little. He could see that this would get pretty tedious after a while. He wanted to get off the table and have another beer. Then he saw Edie looking at him strangely, and then she winked. For a second he thought she was looking at someone else and he had to look again. Sure enough, she was winking and giving him the eye. His spirits rose, and he thought, To hell with it. He pushed his fifty-five pounds on to the square and felt the dealer's eyes jump on him. His heart was racing madly.

The dealer dealt him a ten, and Chris thought okay, as he watched the other cards flash around. The dealer gave himself a ten and Chris's spirits sank a little. Then the dealer dealt him another ten and his heart beat even faster. He was now very close to winning. He watched the other hands being played out and then the dealer dealt to himself. He got a three and a ten, a bust!

Chris nearly punched the air with delight. A few people laughed and made comments, and someone slapped him on the back. Edie was looking at him with a wry smile on her face. He saw £110 worth of chips coming his way. He picked them up and left the table.

When he'd cashed in, he headed for the bar and Edie joined him a few minutes later. He was sipping a celebration bottle of Beck's.

'You're always drinking,' she scolded.

'I think I'm entitled to a little celebration.'

'You should never drink and gamble. I've told you that before.'

'Jesus! We've stopped gambling haven't we? Besides, I've been drinking all evening.'

'You'll have to stop when we start playing as a team. Drink up. I'll wait for you upstairs.'

Chris found her mood swings baffling. A few minutes ago she had been winking at him across the table and now she was back to her businesslike self. What the hell was going on? He decided to let her wait five minutes before leaving. He even tipped the barman a pound.

She was waiting by reception with his coat. She handed it to him, then marched up the stairs to the street and disappeared around a corner. He caught up with her and before he knew it she was hugging him, and planting a big kiss on his lips. He was so shocked he didn't even try to return it.

'That was great!' she said. 'I gave you the signal and you won! It worked! I always knew it would!'

Chris didn't know what she was talking about. 'What do you mean?'

'Come on. Don't play the innocent!'

'I really don't know…'

'I couldn't give you a kiss in there; you never know where they keep cameras. Even in the bars.'

Then Chris understood. Edie's winking had been a sign to lay down a heavy bet. He had thought she was just being friendly. He had only put the money down because he'd had a few beers and was getting bored. He decided to play it cool. 'I suppose that means I'll have to split my winnings with you.'

'Of course it does! I won it for you!'

He held back his disappointment. He took the money out

of his pocket and handed over twenty-five pounds.

'Do you want the two pounds-fifty as well?'

'No, you can keep it. Now let's go and have a drink!'

Chris felt his spirits sinking as she skipped off down the street.

10

AT WORK THE next day, Chris unpacked his weekly delivery of wines and spirits; a task that took up most of the day. He enjoyed dusting the bottles and arranging them on the shelves, filling up gaps that had appeared during the week. Sometimes he wished the shop were his own; then he wouldn't mind putting in such long hours. Maybe if he made some big money at blackjack he could start his own business. Yeah, he thought, and pigs might fly as well.

He thought some more about Edie. Her mood changes were beginning to bother him and he wondered if there was something he was missing. One minute she was cool with him, the next she was planting a big smacker on his lips. What, apart from blackjack, was her game? It was unusual for him to be in a relationship where the woman was in control. He wasn't sure if he liked it or not.

They had only shared one drink after his lucky win, then walked down to Charing Cross together and caught the same train home. Edie had talked mainly about blackjack once again and when Chris left the train at Elmhurst, he'd kissed her on the cheek. Once again she gave an indifferent reaction.

She had, however, said that she wanted to see him again tonight, but rather than looking forward to it, Chris somehow felt that something fishy was in the air. He would have to play it cool until he knew exactly what was going on.

The clock ticked slowly round to eight o'clock. He had a quick wash in the sink in the back room, then locked the shop and started walking towards the West End.

He found Edie waiting for him, punctual as usual, outside the Trocadero. She was wearing jeans today, a cream anorak and trainers. Even dressed down, Chris fancied her. He gave her a kiss on the cheek but again she was about as affectionate as a brick wall.

'So what are we going to do tonight?' he asked.

'I want you to meet someone.'

Chris raised his eyebrows. 'Oh yeah? Well, lead the way.'

They dodged their way through early evening theatre crowds to a pub called The Angel, that Chris had passed about ten minutes ago on his way to meet her. Why couldn't she just have asked to meet him there?

It was a pub Chris had been to many times before, an old-style one with friendly staff, good beer, and none of the trendy trappings of most West End bars. There were office workers crowded inside, so Edie led him out to the small courtyard at the back, where there were wooden tables and benches.

'What would you like?' she asked.

'I'll have a Coke,' Chris said, and Edie looked at him with surprise.

'Are you sure?'

'I had too much last night,' he said. He couldn't be bothered explaining his 'four-day plan'. This being only Tuesday, he didn't want to take up two drinking days, with the rest of the week still to come. That would put him under too much pressure. Besides, he wanted to be sober for this mysterious meeting.

Edie disappeared to the bar and Chris sat down. He felt uneasy by himself and wished he had a newspaper to read. There were four other tables in the yard and all had couples sitting at them. There was a brick wall on two sides of the yard, the pub wall and the men's toilets on the others. Neighbouring buildings overlooked them and the windows of the gents were directly in front of him. Not exactly salubrious surroundings but any open-air area in a central London pub was usually popular.

Edie came back carrying three drinks, one of them a pint of Guinness, a packet of crisps clenched between her teeth. She placed them on the table and Chris asked, 'Why three drinks?'

Edie sat down opposite and opened her crisps. 'Brad's just coming. He's the person I want you to meet.'

'And who's Brad?' Chris asked.

'He's my boyfriend,' Edie said.

Chris felt his stomach lurch. 'Your boyfriend?' he said, a little too loudly. 'You never told me you had a boyfriend.'

'You never asked,' Edie said, looking at him coolly.

Chris didn't know what to say. He felt like a fool. 'So why are you hanging out with me?'

'I told you at the beginning, I need a blackjack partner. I never said I needed anything else.'

Chris had to admit that was true, although he did remember her mention 'dating' the first time they'd gone out. It would also explain why she was so offhand with him most of the time. They fell into an uncomfortable silence until he sensed someone standing beside them. He looked up and saw who he presumed was The Boyfriend.

Edie stood up with a big smile and kissed the man on his lips. Chris forced himself to stand and held out his hand. The Boyfriend was about six foot, a little overweight, short fair hair, with the rough good looks of a Marlboro Man.

'This is Brad,' Edie said. 'Brad, Chris.'

'Pleased to meet you,' Brad said, and Chris was surprised to hear an American accent. But then again, with a name like Brad, what else could he be? They sat down and sipped their drinks.

'So you're the card player,' Brad said. 'I hear you had a good win last night.'

'Just lucky,' Chris shrugged, but then remembered it wasn't meant to have been lucky. 'Well, Edie helped a little too, of course,' he added. Edie smiled.

'She's amazing,' Brad said. 'I played with her a lot when we first met and couldn't believe it.'

'So she recruited you as well?'

'I'm afraid so. Cards always come first with Edie.' He put his arm around her and they both smiled. Chris thought he was going to be sick. What a fool he'd been.

'I have to go to the ladies,' Edie said. 'You two chat a while.'

They both watched her go and then looked at each other.

'So how long have you been going out?' Chris asked.

'Nearly a year,' Brad said. 'We met in Atlantic City when Edie was over on holiday. We were both doing a little gambling there. Then she went home and I followed about five months later. I'm here on a six-month visa but I'm reaching the end of it. Edie has agreed to marry me so I can stay.'

Chris felt his spirits dropping even lower. He really didn't know anything about Edie at all. 'That's nice of her,' he said.

'Don't get me wrong, we're in love with each other. I guess we'd have married eventually. This just brings things forward a few years.'

Chris nodded. He had met a few people over the years who married so their partner could stay in the country. And who was to say it wasn't as good a reason as any? He decided to change the subject. 'So, you used to play cards with her as well?'

'Yeah. When I came over to England we got back into it. I can card count, badly, so I let her do all the work. I was the hammer man, coming in for the big bets. We won a few times but also lost a bit as well, so we stopped doing it. I think she wants to try again with the two of us. Two hammer men are better than one.'

'Come again?'

'She hasn't told you?'

'She's told me she was going to try with me. I didn't know I was going to be part of a team.'

Brad laughed. 'That's Edie for you. Always keeping her cards close to her chest.'

Chris tried to laugh too but found he couldn't. Instead, he sipped his Coke and wondered whether he should just walk away right now and leave them to it. But he actually found himself quite liking this guy. Unlike most Americans, he was softly spoken, and also easy to talk to. Very polite as well, sipping his pint of Guinness.

'Has she told you that Edie isn't her real name?' Brad asked.

Chris shook his head. 'You may as well hit me with all the surprises in one go.'

Brad smiled. 'Her real name is Phyllis. She's always hated the name though, and started calling herself Edie when she was about twenty. She was always a big Paul Newman fan and she became hooked on his films, especially *The Hustler* and then later, *The Color Of Money*. They were both about the same pool hustler. Do you remember what his name was?'

Chris thought back to the two films. He'd seen them both and could remember them quite well. 'Eddie,' he said.

'That's right. Fast Eddie Felson. When Edie started gambling she wanted to take his name. It couldn't be Eddie, of course.'

Chris shook his head. 'It's all starting to make sense. So why did she pick me to become part of her team? I don't have any card-playing experience.'

'She sees something in people. I don't know what exactly, but she does. She saw it in me, but we fell in love. That changed things a bit.'

'I can understand that.'

'You've got classic card-players' eyes,' Brad said. 'Has anyone ever told you that?'

'Never,' Chris said.

'The way you look at people. You're very wary, very watchful, like a wounded animal. It's like you've spent a lifetime at the poker table, glancing over your cards.'

Chris had to smile. Several women in the past had told him he had bedroom eyes, whatever that meant, but this was the first time he'd been told he had poker eyes.

'So, now she's found you,' Brad said, 'I think we're going to make a threesome. If that's all right with you. It could be fun for a while.'

Chris was silent for a moment. He felt like he'd been manipulated. He could always just walk away right now.

'Well, I'll have to think about it. I wish she'd told me all this at the beginning.'

'That's just her way. She's very secretive.'

As if on cue, Edie returned. When she sat down, Brad excused himself for the men's room. They were obviously taking turns with him. It had all been worked out beforehand.

'So what do you think of him?' Edie asked.

'A nice guy,' Chris said. 'I hope you'll both be very happy.'

Edie laughed. 'You're not going to get all bitter on me, are you?'

'No. I just wish you'd told me earlier. I feel like an idiot.'

'I was going to. But I thought you might drop out.'

'And you think I won't drop out now?'

'No. I think you're hooked.'

Chris nodded. He had a feeling she was right. 'So now we split the money three ways? That means we'll have to win a whole lot more.'

'We will win more. I've got a good feeling about this. I think it's all going to work.'

'So is this like your last big score or something? You're going to pull this off and then retire?'

'Something like that. Although I may be too hooked on gambling to give it up entirely.'

'I think you may be, as well.'

Edie leaned closer. 'What I really want the money for, and don't laugh, is for our honeymoon. Brad told you we were getting married?'

'Yes.'

'He doesn't have much money. I want to give him a wedding and honeymoon to remember.'

'That's very sweet of you,' Chris said, unable to keep the sarcasm from his voice. So, he was about to become part of a gambling team to pay for the wedding of the woman he fancied. The whole thing was getting more ludicrous by the minute.

'I'm just an old-fashioned girl at heart,' Edie said.

'I'm sure.'

Then Brad was back to join them, and this time he slapped Chris on the back and sat down next to him. 'So, what do you think?' he asked. 'Are you in or out?'

Chris looked at them both and smiled. 'Oh, I'm definitely in,' he said. 'What else have I got to do with my life?'

They raised their glasses to each other and Edie said, 'To the team.'

'To the team,' Chris and Brad echoed.

11

DAVE BRILL SAT on a roof and looked at the moss. There was plenty of it around on this particular house. Then a tune started forming in his head. Sat on a roof, looked at the moss. Wasn't that a line from a song? He tried remembering which one but the answer wouldn't come. He would have to ask Evelyn tonight. She was always good on old pop songs. One of her few talents.

He was eating one of her cold sausage and tomato sauce sandwiches. How he loved sausage sandwiches. He could eat them all day long. It was a grey day but no sign of rain in the air. Some days he wished it would rain so he could pack up and go home; watch daytime TV instead. It was always nice to have a few unscheduled hours off work.

From this high up he could see into people's back gardens and spy on housewives as they hung out their washing. He preferred sitting on roofs in the summer, because then he might strike lucky and see a woman sunbathing, but at this time of year he just had to make do with their laundry. He tried looking for sexy underwear, but women were generally crafty and kept all that stuff hidden behind sheets or their husband's shirts. Still, it was a challenge, and something to keep him occupied during his lunch break.

For the past seven years, Brill had been a self-employed builder, specialising in chimneys. Before that, he had been a general builder, learning just about everything there was to know about the maintenance of houses, both inside and out. He was pretty useful at painting and decorating, plastering, plumbing and wiring – yet chose to specialise in chimneys because he preferred working outside.

He was now thirty-five and often wondered if the roof-top

life was all he had to look forward to until retirement, at the age of sixty-five. Another thirty years! It wasn't a bad job exactly, just very repetitive, like all building work soon became. In the early days he had worked with a radio next to him, but nowadays he preferred working in silence, except for the occasional mutterings of his hired hand, Luke Tremble, who wasn't exactly the greatest conversationalist in the world. He could see Luke now, down below, eating a sandwich and reading the *Sun*. Brill tore a piece of bread off and threw it down at him. It hit Luke's paper but he just brushed it away and didn't even look up. Brill took a bite from his sandwich. Even Luke was treating him with indifference.

There was a flask of tea balanced next to him and Brill poured himself a cup. He started thinking about Chris Small and how he could wheedle his way into his life, maybe cause him a bit of bother for damage done in the past. That would be something to take his mind off boring, everyday routine.

About seven years ago, Brill had been the neighbour of Kevin Jenkins, a young man who'd ended up dead thanks to the antics of Chris Small. Kevin lived with his father Basil, and although their relationship was sometimes volatile, Brill had got on well with them both, and often used Basil's electrical shop for his building supplies.

Brill had read about Kevin's death in the local paper and, after offering his condolences, had visited the off-licence in Boroughheath where Small worked, just to see what he looked like.

In the months that followed, Basil had struggled to come to terms with the death of his only son, and Brill could still remember the anguished look on his face, together with the defeated stoop in his walk. About a year later, he had driven his car to Beachy Head one evening, parked near the cliffs and walked off into the air. He was found the next morning, his body smashed to pieces on the rocks.

So, together with the death, also by suicide, of a friend of Kevin's called Leo Dash, Brill reckoned Chris Small was responsible for the deaths of three people – and he was still walking the streets. Some things in life just weren't fair. Brill would like to ask Small about his past and how he lived with it. Did he have trouble sleeping at night and did it ever get on his conscience? It would be interesting finding out.

He looked down at Luke. Now there was another nutter he couldn't understand. He thought of a story that Luke had told him recently.

A couple of years ago, Luke had been sitting in a pub on a Monday evening, watching Arsenal on Sky TV. He'd left the pub a couple of minutes before the end because his beloved Arsenal had been losing one-nil. On the train ride back to London where he lived, the effects of a hard day's work and about five pints of beer had made Luke feel a bit sleepy. The train had been packed with families and tourists, so to get some peace he had stepped into a first-class carriage and fallen asleep. He had been woken up a little later by a ticket collector, questioning whether he was in the right part of the train.

When Luke had dug out his second-class ticket a loud argument had followed, and a few moments later Luke snapped, grabbing the man by the coat and throwing him on the seat. He had punched him a few times in the face then turned around to see several people watching from the corridor. One of them, a strong looking guy well over six feet tall, had kept his hand on the sliding door so Luke couldn't escape, and at the next station he'd been arrested.

In a London police station, Luke had been put in a cell to cool down. When questioned later by two policemen he was asked what had made him so violent? Luke had replied, 'The Arsenal defeat.'

The two policemen looked at him with puzzled expressions. 'What Arsenal defeat?'

Luke said, 'The one this evening.'

The policemen looked at each other and shook their heads. 'Arsenal didn't lose,' one of them said. 'They scored twice in the last two minutes, to win the match.'

After his trial, Luke spent three months locked up in Maidstone jail. It was all so futile and the only thing it had taught him was to never leave a match before the end.

Sitting on the roof now, Brill felt there was no justice in the world. Luke had done time for beating up a ticket collector, while Chris Small, with three deaths connected to him, had done no time at all. Where was the logic in that?

He could still remember from the local paper how Small had received a suspended sentence. Okay, so he hadn't landed the blow that had caused the death of Kevin Jenkins, but he had arranged the whole scam that had made Leo Dash land the blow, which had then brought on the suicides of Leo and Basil. He should have got more than just a suspended sentence. The whole system was arse over tit, but you didn't need to be a rocket scientist to figure that one out.

Brill finished his sandwiches and tea. He looked at the chimney next to him and figured that, in a couple of hours, he could go home. The rebuilding had all been finished, now they could start on the rendering. That was one good thing about his job, he could work the hours he wanted. Go as fast or as slow as he wished.

He looked down at Luke and called to him, 'Are you ready, young man?'

Luke closed his paper and gave him the thumbs up.

When Luke got sick of working with him, Brill thought, he would make sure his next helper spoke at least a few words of decent conversation. It would make the day go faster, at least.

12

THE SUNDAY AFTER the threesome had been formed, Chris was sitting in Edie and Brad's flat in Orpington, learning all about card counting. Not that he was going to learn how to count, he just wanted to get the general idea. He was still going to let Edie do all of the hard work.

The off-licence was being run by Hugh Blake, his first Sunday alone. After working with Chris last Sunday, Hugh had come in one day during the week to pick up a set of keys and see how the alarm worked. He had also filled some shelves and dusted, had another go on the till, and acted happy and relaxed about the whole set-up. Chris had congratulated himself on such a good choice. It was nice to have two days off in a row, his first for six months.

'Let's recap a little,' Edie said. They were sitting at a small dining table in the living room. Brad was in the kitchen, cooking Sunday lunch. 'The Basic Strategy player, i.e. you, over a course of time, will still lose ten pounds for every thousand he puts down. You'll still be a better player than nine out of ten people who sit at a table but, you'll agree, that losing that small amount for such a lot of effort isn't really worth it. You may as well put your money in a building society.'

'Agreed,' Chris said. It felt good being in someone else's flat. When was the last time he'd been invited for Sunday lunch? He couldn't remember. It was a nice flat too, on three different levels. Brad and Edie rented it from an Irish couple who were getting divorced, and they'd left most of the furniture behind. In this room there was a sofa and armchair, a TV and video on a small black stand, and a dining table with four chairs. There was a small bookshelf with mainly card-playing books on it, and by the TV set there were about twenty videos.

Chris had noticed earlier that there were several on how to play poker and blackjack.

'Now the only way to change this,' Edie continued, 'is to know what cards are coming next. Or rather, when to know that the deck is in your favour. You'll never know exactly what's coming next, unless you play with transparent cards.'

'They have transparent cards?'

'That was a joke,' Edie said.

'Right.' Chris was finding it hard to concentrate. Edie was wearing a pink T-shirt and he was sure there was no bra underneath. His eyes kept straying downwards.

'Now the way we do this is to give each card a value. There are lots of different counting systems but I'm just going to run through The Main Count System.' Edie placed a card on the table in front of him. 'In The Main Count System, these are the values we give to cards.'

Chris looked at the card. It read:

Card	2	3	4	5	6	7	8	9	10	ace
Point Count	+1	+1	+2	+2	+2	+1	0	0	- 2	-1

'As cards are being dealt, you keep a Running Count in your head using these figures. When the Running Count is high, i.e. lots of those high scoring cards have been dealt, it means that there are some good cards coming your way and you should raise your bets. If the reverse is true, then you lower your bets.'

'And you find you can keep track of this?'

'It takes practice but it's possible. You have to concentrate though. That's why I don't talk to anyone at the table. I have to cocoon myself. It does, however, get more difficult.'

'I thought it might.'

'This would work easily if the casinos only played with one deck of cards. Unfortunately, in Britain, most of them play with six.'

'Do they play with less in America?'

'It varies from town to town, and from casino to casino.

You can get one deck, two, four, six, or even eight. The good card counter will have a slightly different strategy for each and can adapt his play. I'm not up to that standard yet so I just stick with the six decks.'

'So what happens?'

'You have to find out what the True Count is.'

'The True Count?'

'Yes.'

'This is getting complicated.'

'It is at first. That's why you won't be doing any counting.'

Chris forced a laugh. Edie could be very blunt sometimes. He wondered if she knew she was. 'Well, lay it on me.'

'Say we're playing with six decks. You have to estimate how many decks have been dealt already. You can do this by judging how thick the pile of used cards is. They're always sitting on the table next to the dealer. So if there are approximately three decks left to be dealt, you divide the Running Count by three and that gives you your True Count. If there are two packs left, you divide by two and that gives you your True Count. It's obviously a lot better for you if there are hardly any cards left and you have a high count of, say, plus fifteen, than if you have plus fifteen and there are still three packs to be dealt. What would the True Count be then?'

'If you have plus fifteen and three packs still to be dealt?'

'Yes.'

'Your True Count would be plus five.'

Edie nodded. 'We'll make a card counter of you yet.'

Chris smiled. 'So how would I learn to card count?'

'Very slowly.' Edie produced a pack of cards. 'You would have to start off with just one pack and deal them out, keeping a Running Count. When you come to the end of the pack your score should always be zero.'

'Always zero?'

'Every time. Remember, you always see all the cards in blackjack. It's not like poker. Therefore, your count should be accurate.'

'Okay.'

'So you practice this over and over, until you can count one deck in about thirty seconds.'

'Christ! That's quick.'

'Thirty seconds is what you should be aiming for.'

'That sounds like a lot of work.'

'You always have to work at things. A quicker way to do it is to group cards together.' Edie placed another numbered table in front of him. 'If you look at this table, a 4, 4 and a 6 come to +6. A 5, 3 and ace come to +2. If you learn little groups like this it'll be quicker, rather than just one by one.'

Chris nodded. 'It certainly doesn't look easy. I think I'll leave it to you.'

'You will be doing, don't worry.'

'It's interesting to know what you've had to learn though. It must have taken ages.'

Edie nodded. 'I was doing about four hours a day to start with. Now I have to do about an hour, just to keep my brain in tune.'

'You're more dedicated than I'd ever be.'

'When you've learnt to count one pack, you start adding more packs. At the end, you should be able to do four packs in around two minutes.'

'Two minutes! Jesus.'

Edie smiled. 'You have to be that quick. In a casino there'll be distractions. The cards will be coming thick and fast. There'll be lots of other players around talking, smoking, being a general pain. If you lose concentration, then there goes your count.'

'So what happens then?'

'If you lose it, you can either revert to Basic Strategy until the new shoe starts, or just get up and leave the table. That's the beauty of blackjack.'

'What?'

'You can get up and leave when you want. Take a breather. Come back when you're ready for a fresh count. You can play when you want to. The dealer has to play all the time. He can't just stop. You can just march in, start counting, and leave when you want. Another little edge for you.'

'Okay. And that's about it?'

'Not quite.'

'I need another beer.'

'Brad's got some more.'

'How about you?'

'I'll have another cup of tea.'

Chris took their empties to the kitchen. It was up a few stairs, on another level. Brad was sitting at the table, reading a Sunday paper. 'Having fun?' he asked.

'Bunches,' Chris said. 'Now I know why you gave up on card counting. It's doing my head in.'

Brad nodded. 'It's too hard. I don't have the drive or the memory.'

'I haven't told Edie yet that I've always been lousy at maths.'

They both laughed.

'We need another cup of tea and another beer.'

'Help yourself.'

Back in the living room, Edie told Chris all about betting strategy, but things were getting too complicated. His brain was starting to get fuzzy. He was on his third bottle of beer and all he wanted to do was crash out on the sofa, preferably with Edie in his arms. He tuned himself out as she showed him diagrams from a book called *The Money-Spinners*, by someone who called himself Jacques Black. The diagrams reminded him of maths lessons at school. It was amazing how these gamblers analysed everything; but then again, if you were playing for serious money, or for a living, you would have to. He tuned himself back in.

'A man using this betting system with a £10,000 bankroll, playing for £25 a hand, would have to play six hours every day for forty days to win another £10,000,' Edie said.

Chris worked it out. 'A month and a third. That's not bad money.'

'No, but six hours a day would fry your brain.'

'Still, you could do it for less. You could still earn fifty grand a year quite easily.'

'Theoretically, yes. But you have to do all this without getting caught. Also, in card counting you have to be prepared for long losing streaks. Sometimes you'll be doing everything right and still losing. It's a tough way to make a living.'

Brad came into the room and said, 'Can we eat now? It'll spoil if we wait much longer.'

Edie turned and smiled at him. 'You're so domesticated,' she said.

They ate in the kitchen, the table already laid by Brad. He carved some roast beef, and they helped themselves to potatoes and vegetables. There were two open bottles of red wine. Chris was surprised. He hadn't seen either of them drink in large quantities yet. Maybe they would loosen up and he'd find out some of their secrets. Hopefully the conversation would get away from gambling for a while, but he wasn't counting on it.

'So tell me, Brad,' Chris said when they were eating, 'what kind of film will you direct when you eventually get round to it?' He had found out at their first meeting that Brad had a degree in film studies from a university in New Jersey. At the moment, though, he was working in a photocopying shop near New Oxford Street.

Brad laughed, not knowing whether he was joking or not. 'I like small films. The independents. I'm not interested in Hollywood blockbusters.'

Chris gave him a puzzled look. 'Name me some and I'll tell you if I've seen them.'

'Okay,' Brad said. 'Have you heard of a director called Hal Hartley?'

Chris shook his head. 'I don't pay much attention to directors. Just tell me some titles.'

'Okay,' Brad said. 'He did *Simple Men,* plus another two. I can't think of their titles at the moment.' He looked at Edie for help.

'Me neither,' she said. 'Have you heard of a film called *Hard Eight*? That's an independent. It was all about gambling.'

'Can't say that I have,' Chris said, despondent that Edie had already turned the conversation back to her favourite subject.

'The Coen brothers,' Brad said. 'Films like *Blood Simple* and *Fargo*. Have you seen those?'

'I've seen *Fargo*. A great film.'

'Okay.' Brad paused to think. '*Trees Lounge*. That was a good one. *Flirting With Disaster. The Sweet Hereafter. The Daytrippers. The Brothers McMullen*?'

'I've seen *The Brothers McMullen*,' Chris said. 'I liked that one.'

Brad nodded. 'Well, that sort of thing. Small budget, well-written. They don't make a lot of money but they're much more satisfying to watch. *Reservoir Dogs* and *sex, lies and videotape*. Now they're two obvious ones.'

'I'm getting the idea,' Chris said. 'And have you written anything yet?'

'I've written a screenplay.'

'What's it about?'

'Gambling,' Edie interjected. 'Funnily enough.'

Chris decided he wasn't going to be put off by Edie's one-track mind. 'And what will you do while Brad's on the film set all day?'

Edie shrugged. 'Go gambling. If Brad's in LA, it's not too far from Vegas.'

'So you plan to live in LA?'

'Maybe,' Brad said. 'You've got to live where the work is, but that's a long way down the line. We have to get married first.' He squeezed one of Edie's hands.

Chris felt slightly jealous that Edie would be whisked away, out of his reach. But did he really have anything in common with her anyway? He decided to jump in at the deep end. 'Tell me something about your childhood, Edie. I don't know much about you at all.'

Edie looked at him with a straight face, then much to Chris's surprise started talking. 'My parents owned a hotel in Torquay. That's where I was brought up. I left school at the age of sixteen because I wasn't getting anywhere. I was good at maths but nothing else. I just wanted to get out and earn some money so I worked for my parents for a couple of years. Then, when I was eighteen, I went to work in various pubs and restaurants. Then I left Torquay.' She shrugged.

'No brothers or sisters?'

Edie shook her head. 'None.'

Chris felt as if he'd made a small breakthrough. At last he knew a little more about Edie.

'The only thing I miss about Torquay,' she continued, 'is the riding.'

'The riding?' Chris asked.

'I used to go horse riding as a child. I was pretty good at it. Whenever I go home, I visit the local stables and go out for an hour or two. I'd like to own a horse someday.'

'Plenty of room in America,' Chris said.

'That's what I'm hoping for.'

'Edie was obviously born in the wrong era,' Brad said. 'She should've been a cowgirl.'

Chris nodded. 'She should have. Riding and gambling. The two go together.'

Edie smiled. She obviously liked the idea.

Chris wondered if he'd been born in the wrong era too. Sometimes he felt as if he were living in a different world to everyone else. It was something he'd have to put some thought to. Along with seeing some more independent films.

After lunch, the three of them sat around the table and worked out what hand signals to use when they played as a team. Edie got out her Ken Uston book and showed them the different ways. They could use any signals they wanted, as long as they were subtle and easy to see. In the end, they settled on Edie giving them signs with the fingers of her left hand. They played for a few hours, until they thought they had it working smoothly.

At six o'clock, Chris went home, feeling a little light-headed from the booze and a little depressed as it wore off. Edie said she'd ring him for their next casino outing. She had been impressed that he'd bought a computer game to practise with. She told him to keep at it. She told him to keep notes. Write down how many hands he won and lost, how many he pushed, and see how the odds always worked slightly against the Basic Strategy player.

So that's what he did. He went back home, sat in his silent room and switched on his laptop.

13

THE COMPUTER GAME Chris used only cost him fifteen pounds and he reckoned it was money well spent. He could learn everything he needed to know about blackjack, including card counting. He wasn't going to get into that just yet, but it was handy knowing it was there, and he would rather learn it on computer than from a book or with a pack of cards.

For brushing up his Basic Strategy, he set the options at the six-deck game and then sat with a pad of paper and recorded every move. A computer voice told him if he'd made the wrong play and what the right one was. It was fun seeing how many plays he could make before getting one wrong. It didn't matter if he won or lost the hand, just so long as he made the right move. Doing it this way made him worry less about the money and more about the strategy, which he figured was the right thing to do. If he got his strategy down faultless then the money would take care of itself.

When he'd first bought the game he was getting up to about ten hands without making a wrong move, and then stretched it to twenty. After a week, he was hardly making any wrong plays at all, about two or three every sixty hands. He was winning most of the time, mostly small amounts, betting ten dollars every hand. Some days he was over the hundred-dollar mark for winnings, and he reckoned if he halved that into pounds then that would be what he could expect to win in a London casino.

Sometimes he lost heavily though, and he found it was a lot easier losing large amounts than it was winning them. He found this worrying, but would have to know when he was on a losing streak and just leave the table. He came to realise that Edie was right. There was no long-term future in Basic Strategy, and if he wanted to win regularly he would have to learn to count. But Basic was okay for now. He would let Edie do all the hard work and wait for her signals.

According to Edie's casino directory, there were twenty-two casinos in London. Six of these she had crossed off, either because they had an annual membership fee, an entrance fee, or they required you to wear elegant dress. Edie wasn't into the snob value of gambling; getting dressed to the nines and pretending to be a high roller. All she wanted was to get their money, then get out quick. So, over the years, she had joined the sixteen others, and had their different colour membership cards stuck inside her credit-card holder.

As Chris went round with her over the next few weeks – always fairly late in the evenings after work – he joined the casinos he liked; the ones where he felt most at ease. They went to casinos in Curzon Street, Baker Street, Berkeley Square, Kensington High Street, Russell Square and Cromwell Road. Sometimes they did three in an evening, other times only one. Each time, Chris stuck to his Basic Strategy and just about broke even all the time, while Edie usually came out with small winnings. He kept looking at the croupiers, floor managers, and pit bosses to see if they were noticing Edie counting cards, but because she was young and good-looking – and also didn't bet heavy amounts – she seemed to go unnoticed.

Chris also watched the croupiers as they watched the players, and felt there was a heavy dose of contempt on their side. And how could they feel anything else? For here was this group of punters sitting in front of them, most of whom didn't know how to play the game properly, slapping down money as if there were no tomorrow, trusting blindly to lady luck. Only a fool would part with his money so easily.

After a while, Chris found it all a bit tedious, but it was better than staying in his room and he knew that Brad was going to join them soon. He spent a few more Sundays with the two of them, going over the signals, getting everything worked out. He was looking forward to playing as a threesome. Things would really start getting interesting then.

*

March turned to April and Chris started feeling more optimistic about life. Because of the blackjack playing, his alcohol intake had been cut, and he found himself feeling better than he had done for years. Maybe non-drinkers had something. Maybe drinking really was a waste of time.

He was sitting at home one evening, practising, when the front doorbell rang. He nearly fell off the bed, so rarely did he have visitors. He put on his slippers and made the long walk downstairs.

He opened the front door to find a stocky man, probably in his mid-thirties, standing there. He had cropped hair, and stubble all over his cheeks. He was wearing an anorak and dark blue tracksuit bottoms; trainers on his feet.

'Evening,' the man said. 'Are you Mr Small?'

'That's right,' Chris said.

'My name's Dave Brill. I've been sent by your landlord to check out your windows. Now that winter's over he wants to see if they're all right. No cracks or such; paintwork still okay.'

Chris immediately felt wary. 'He never told me he was sending anyone over. In fact, he lives in Spain.'

The man seemed taken aback for a second. 'I know that. He e-mailed me this morning. Asked me to pop round.'

'Are you sure?'

'Sure as sure can be. His name's Packard, right?'

Chris nodded. Packard lived in Spain and his ex-wife picked up the rent each week. She was a dour, unsmiling woman who Chris had only met a few times. Maybe this guy was on the level. How else would he know Packard's name? 'So he wants you to check the windows? He's never had anything checked since I've been here. Have you got some ID or something?'

The man reached in his anorak and brought out a card. Chris looked at it. It said 'David Brill' and had 'General Building Maintenance' written underneath, with an address in Sidcup, and two phone numbers.

'Can you wait here a minute?' Chris said. 'We were burgled last month so I'm not going to let just anyone in. I'll check with the other tenants and see if they know anything.'

The man looked at him with an annoyed expression. 'Ask if you like. I'll be waiting.'

Chris shut the door and walked upstairs to John's room. He knocked and John opened the door.

'There's a man downstairs,' Chris said, 'who reckons he's been sent by Mr Packard to check our windows. Do you know anything about it?'

'It's the first I've heard,' John said.

'Me too. I'm reluctant to let him in after what happened last month. He also looks a bit scary; like Ross Kemp.'

'Who's Ross Kemp?'

'He played a baddie on *EastEnders*. One of the Mitchell brothers.'

'I never watch *EastEnders*. In fact, I don't watch anything any more. No TV.'

'I know what you mean. So what do you reckon?'

'I reckon, fuck him. For all we know he might be ringing doorbells to see if anyone's in, prior to coming in himself. And why would he be coming round at this time of night?'

Chris nodded. He was shocked to hear John swear. He'd never heard a foul word escape his lips before. 'Have you bought a new stereo yet?' he asked.

'I can't afford one. I'm going crazy in here. I miss my country music.'

Chris felt sorry for him. 'Me neither. I'm playing computer games instead. They missed my laptop in the wardrobe.'

'Bastards.'

'Well, I'll send him packing then. See you later.'

Chris went back downstairs. There was music coming from Heavy Metal's room – unfortunately he had quickly bought a new sound system – but he couldn't be bothered asking him. He'd probably be out of his head on some illegal substance anyway.

Chris opened the front door but the man was gone. He stepped outside and looked down the road. Just as he thought. Another fucking troublemaker. He looked at the man's card. Well at least he knew his name.

He shut the door and went back upstairs. He kicked off his slippers, sat on the bed, and picked up his laptop. But he couldn't concentrate on Basic Strategy any more. He stood up and made himself a cup of tea instead.

14

DAVE BRILL WALKED back to his car and climbed in. He wasn't too upset about not getting into Chris Small's flat. At least he'd spoken to him and made his presence felt. Now he could start pestering him regularly and see what happened. Give the bastard the payback that was long overdue.

He drove his black BMW 520I along the streets, revelling once more in the luxury of the leather seats. From the steering-wheel controls, he turned on the six-rack CD player, pressed the shuffle button and waited to see what happened. A second later, Rod Stewart came on singing 'I Was Only Joking' and Brill was in seventh heaven. He always had at least one Rod Stewart CD in the rack, and one by Phil Collins. As far as he was concerned, they were the two gods of British rock.

Brill had bought the BMW six months ago for £25,000, after saving for years, and it was always a pleasure to drive. It was his little treat to himself and meant Evelyn could have the Vauxhall Vectra for herself and the kids. Tony and Joanna were banned from the BMW for the foreseeable future; he didn't want them messing up the Montana upholstery with their crisps and chocolates. It was far too expensive for that.

The Brill family lived in a three-bedroom detached house on a semi-circular estate in Sidcup. Brill had bought the house soon after Basil Jenkins' suicide, when he'd felt that living next to a house of death was maybe not a healthy idea. With a baby on the way as well, Evelyn had been easily persuaded, so the new house was bought and moved to within a couple of months. The kids had a room each, while Brill shared the main bedroom with Evelyn.

To the outside world they were the typical two-kids, two-car family, but there was a little secret that Brill had been keeping from Evelyn for the past couple of years. Her name was Rosetta and she was the sexiest woman he had ever known.

Rosetta also lived in Sidcup, just a few minutes' drive from Brill's house. They had met when he was doing some chimney work for her, and she'd flirted outrageously with him. It was every builder's fantasy to have sex with a lady whose house they were repairing, but in Brill's experience the opportunities were few and far between. So when this one had arisen with Rosetta, he had grabbed it, and her, with both hands. He reckoned it was just reward for all the long hours he put in, in all kinds of weather.

There was an old Clint Eastwood and Jeff Bridges movie that Brill liked, called *Thunderbolt and Lightfoot,* and it had one scene that he'd always been obsessed with. Jeff Bridges was working in a garden one day when the lady of the house suddenly appeared stark naked at the window, smoking a cigarette. Bridges hadn't taken the matter any further, but the scene had always stayed with Brill until Rosetta did exactly the same thing to him. He had been clearing his gear away at the end of the day, when he'd looked up and there she was, stark naked at the window and looking right at him. And then she'd crooked her finger, beckoning him inside.

When Brill had walked into the living room in his scruffy clothes, Rosetta had quickly stripped him naked, then run her tongue down the entire length of his sweaty body. They had fucked wildly on the sofa, and afterwards Rosetta suggested they shower together but Brill had declined. It would look too suspicious if he returned home clean and tidy.

The affair had carried on ever since, two or three times a week. Rosetta was divorced and in her mid-fifties. She had long, dyed-blonde hair, and a lovely slim figure. Her eyes were deep-set and she had high cheekbones. On days when she wore dark eye-liner she could look quite evil, but once he got to know her, and when she was naked underneath him, she was as soft, tender and affectionate as he could wish any woman to be. She knew how to use her slim fingers, and her long nails drove him to the brink of madness nearly every time. She had awoken a virility in him that had been dormant for years. He'd had two years of great sex and no ties. What more could any man want?

He parked the BMW in the street outside her house, walked up the driveway and unlocked the front door. He'd had his own key for some time now and Rosetta didn't care about the neighbours or what they thought.

He found her in the living room watching TV, drinking her usual gin and tonic. She was wearing black slacks and a dark green blouse. She was stretched out on the sofa, long and lean, and he bent down and kissed her on the cheek. She didn't even look at him.

'What's this rubbish?' he asked.

'Don't know,' she said. 'I've just turned it on. Where have you been? You were meant to be here an hour ago.'

'I had something to do.'

She looked at him for the first time. 'I don't want to get possessive with you, Dave, you know I'm not that kind, but I do expect you to be punctual. I made supper and it's past its best now.'

'Sorry. But I really did have something to do. Let's eat and I'll tell you all about it.'

They walked through to the kitchen, where the table was laid for two. Brill put himself to use by opening a bottle of red wine.

As they ate he told her all about Chris Small and Boroughheath, and the three deaths that he reckoned Small was responsible for. But when he'd finished Rosetta just said 'So what?' and Brill couldn't believe what he'd heard.

'What do you mean, so what?' he said. 'This guy is responsible for three deaths. Don't you think he deserves a little payback?'

'I'm not sure,' Rosetta said. 'If Leo Dash hadn't mugged him in the first place, then none of it would have happened. It wasn't his fault he got involved with a couple of thugs. He was only getting his own kind of revenge.'

'Yeah, but he got away with it. I don't think it's fair.'

Rosetta reached out and patted his hand. 'Very few things in life are, dear. I think you're blowing it all out of proportion. It's not your problem. What sort of penance do you want him to pay, anyway?'

Brill had to think about that one. He didn't know himself. 'Maybe I'd just like to beat him up. A guy like that deserves a beating.'

Rosetta mimed a yawn. 'Oh, so macho. Excuse me if I'm not impressed.'

Brill felt himself getting angry. 'Women don't understand these things anyway. It's a man thing. One against one.'

Rosetta shook her head and stood up. 'I'm going to wash the dishes. You can sit there and be macho.'

Brill had a few drinks and watched while Rosetta splashed at the sink. Her ex-husband was a wealthy banker who worked in London. She had filed for divorce after he'd drifted home late, one too many evenings, with the smell of perfume on his shirt. He had sold their five-bedroom house near Bromley, bought himself a flat in the Docklands, and Rosetta this two-bedroom place. He sent her a monthly cheque – Rosetta had never told Brill how much – while he screwed all the office pussy he could find. Both of them were a lot happier that way, although Brill felt Rosetta drank too much. But what else did she have to do with her time? Apart from satisfy his needs. He wondered how she'd ever survived without him.

After washing the dishes, Rosetta slumped in front of the TV with a drink and didn't speak to him. Brill felt more than a little horny but was too scared to make a move. Eventually he got up to leave and kissed her on the cheek.

'Goodbye, macho man,' she said, and Brill wondered why she was taking this so badly. Was it all because he'd been an hour late? He would come back in a few days when she'd had time to cool down.

He felt in a bad mood as he drove home. He felt that women didn't understand these things. It was in a man's nature to have the occasional brawl and he believed it could sometimes do you good. It helped put things in perspective. But then again, when had he ever been in a fight? He had to think about that one. The last time had probably been at school, when he'd gone to help a friend who was being set upon in the playground by five or six others. Brill had run to his rescue and had ended up with a black eye and a cut lip. But it had made him feel better, and the friend had been grateful, too. And his attackers had treated him with respect afterwards, as well. It had been a positive experience all round.

It was only nine o'clock when he got home and Evelyn, exactly like Rosetta, was slumped in front of the TV with a drink. Unlike Rosetta though, she looked up at him.

'You're home early,' she said.

'Luke had to go home. We had a bite and that was it.' Luke had become his permanent excuse for his nights with Rosetta. Evelyn had only met Luke a few times and Brill always primed him if he needed to lie. Luke was usually so quiet, though, that Evelyn didn't bother making conversation, so he was the perfect alibi. She often asked Brill how he could spend so much social time with a mute. Brill just replied that Luke was more talkative once you got to know him. He had hidden depths. Evelyn could never quite get her head round that one, though.

He sat down beside her on the sofa and looked her over. He was feeling frustrated from not getting his leg over with Rosetta but could he be bothered having sex with his wife? He had to do it at least once a month just to keep her happy. But was tonight going to be that night?

Evelyn was dressed in black leggings and a pink sweatshirt. He could never figure out why it was always fat women who wore leggings. Didn't they realise they looked awful in them? His wife's bum was far too big for his liking and her breasts were huge and sagging. Some nights she was okay to fool around with, though. It could be fun bouncing up and down on all that flesh if he'd had a few drinks. And he'd had a few tonight.

'Fancy fooling around?' he asked.

Evelyn looked at him and smiled. 'It's my time of the month.'

'You know I don't mind the blood,' he said.

Evelyn thought about it for a few seconds. 'Well, go and wash your hands first. I don't want a repeat of last time.'

Brill got up and went to the kitchen to wash. The last time they'd made love had been after they'd both been preparing supper a few weeks ago. Brill had been cutting chillies that evening and neglected to wash afterwards. When his hands had wandered down Evelyn's pants she'd started feeling burning sensations down below. Neither of them knew what the matter was until the pain was too much and Evelyn had to go to the bathroom to wash. Brill had smelt his fingers and then remembered that you should always wash your hands after cutting chilli because the fire still lingers. He chuckled at the memory. Even though he had been nowhere near a chilli tonight, Evelyn obviously still didn't trust him. He dried his hands and walked back to the living room, feeling horny.

Evelyn tossed back her drink and stood up enthusiastically. 'I'll go and get a towel,' she said.

'Make sure it's a red one,' Brill said, as he turned off the TV and dimmed the lights.

15

BY THE END of April it was time for Brad to make up the threesome. Chris and Edie had done the rounds of all the casinos they were going to use and now it was time to put the team into action.

The casino they picked was The Majestic in Russell Square; it was a fifteen-minute walk from the Trocadero and only a five-minute walk from Chris's shop. They chose it because it wasn't as crowded as the West End casinos, so they could concentrate on what they were doing.

Chris was eager to get started and see what would happen. He shut the shop on a Tuesday evening and walked to Russell Square. He was a member of The Majestic so he was going to meet the other two inside. He signed himself in at the door and went to sit at the bar.

The Majestic was better known for its poker room and was considered to be the best in London for that particular game. Poker wasn't catered for in Britain as much as it was in America, simply because it was impossible for casinos to make serious money from it. British casinos were notorious for their attitude towards profit and putting the customer last, and that's why there were only two casinos in London that had decent poker rooms; this one and The Albert in Edgware Road. Chris thought about this as he sat at the bar with a Coke. It was amazing the things he was learning about gambling. Soon he would be able to bore the socks off anyone who asked.

About ten minutes later he saw Edie walk in, followed a few minutes later by Brad. Both were dressed in smart casuals; Edie in her blue blouse and black skirt, Brad in black corduroy trousers and a white shirt. They looked at him and made eye contact but didn't smile or wave. That was part of the plan. They were all to act like total strangers.

Chris watched them walk separately into the casino area, then finished his Coke and did the same.

The Majestic was similar to the other casinos Chris had been in: small and smoky, with predominantly red furnishings. He walked around looking at the various tables. At this time of the evening the place was barely a quarter full. There was a hotel next door and Chris presumed most of the gamblers were staying there. The surrounding area was also full of hotels.

He spotted Brad walking around, trying to look nonchalant. Chris thought he looked too obvious and felt very conspicuous himself, although he was probably just being paranoid. Having an empty casino for easier betting conditions also meant that mixing in with the crowd was harder, because there was no crowd to mix in with. He wondered if Edie had thought about that. He would mention it to her later.

Edie was already sitting at a blackjack table, playing quietly. There were a few other people to her right, and Chris saw Brad walk over and sit on her left as planned. Chris did one more circuit of the room then went to sit at Brad's left, leaving one empty seat between them.

The plan was to play Basic Strategy until Edie gave them a hand signal. Brad and Chris could afford to relax and chat to the dealer, although Chris preferred staying quiet until he gained more experience. He listened to Brad playing the part of a loud, obnoxious, slightly drunk American; a plan that was meant to divert attention from Edie and make Brad's winnings, if he got any, seem more like luck than skill.

The cards flashed round for ten or fifteen minutes while Chris and Brad waited for the signal. Edie was playing with both her hands on the table and the signal for them to raise their bets was simply for her to tuck the small finger of her left hand into her palm. They could watch her hand easily, and they were looking in the direction they should be looking, so how could a pit boss notice anything fishy?

Eventually the signal came and Chris felt his heart rush. He put two five-pound chips in front of him, while noticing that Brad had laid down three and Edie had stuck to one. The plan was for Edie to bet flat all the time; if they all started laying heavy bets it would be too obvious.

Brad started getting intentionally louder. He was making comments on virtually every hand and Chris could sense the dealer getting irritated. But that was all part of the plan.

The money for tonight had been taken from Edie's bankroll. Chris had a hundred pounds in his pocket, Brad two, Edie her usual hundred. Chris felt a lot better knowing the money wasn't his but was disappointed when he lost the first hand. He was relieved, however, to see that Brad had won.

Edie kept her finger tucked under for the next five hands and, during that time, Chris reckoned he won around fifty pounds while Brad won a lot more. Then Edie leant back in her chair and put her hands in her lap.

A pit boss had appeared behind the dealer, and Chris knew that Edie leaning back was the sign for Brad to lose a few hands on purpose. He watched him throw a few chips down, make a few bad calls, and lose some of his winnings. Almost immediately, the pit boss moved away. Chris almost chuckled out loud. Was it going to be as easy as this every time?

They played on a bit longer, had one more sign from Edie that lasted about ten minutes, and then one by one left the table and casino separately.

They met in a bar called Deans, a hundred yards down the road. Chris walked in and found the two of them at the same table, a pint of bitter waiting for him. He sat down and smiled. 'Like taking candy from a baby.'

'It was, it was!' Edie said, excitedly. 'It all went so smoothly, even when that pit boss came over.'

Chris reached over and patted Brad on the shoulder. 'This man is a natural actor. You were great!'

'Thanks,' Brad said smiling. 'But you must know us

Americans are better actors than you Brits.'

Chris nearly choked on his beer. 'I'll let that one slide.'

They relived it all again and got another round of drinks. They wanted to take out their money and count it in the pub but there was no way they were going to do that; Edie and Brad would count it when they got home.

'So where do we hit next?' Chris asked.

'Let me think about it,' Edie said. 'We won't be able to go back there for a few weeks. Give that pit boss time to forget us. We may even have to wear a bit of disguise next time.'

'Disguise? Like what?'

'I look very good in a dark wig,' Edie said. 'And Brad looks totally different in his glasses and a suit. You'll have to think of something, too.'

Chris laughed. 'Maybe I could grow a beard.'

'Maybe a false one,' Brad said. 'Or a moustache.'

'Jesus. I don't know if I could keep a straight face.'

'You could if thousands of pounds were coming your way,' Edie said. 'And hopefully they will. As we gain more confidence we'll up our bets.'

Chris couldn't believe all this was happening. Here he was, sitting in a pub with two people he barely knew, thinking of ways to scam London casinos out of their money. Who'd have thought a couple of months ago that this would be his new pastime?

They left Deans after the second drink and walked back to Charing Cross station. On the way, Chris emptied his pockets and handed all his money over. He would find out later how much they'd made; it wasn't that important for now. Edie handed him fifty pounds for his night's work.

'Thanks,' Chris said. 'I don't feel as if I deserve it.'

'You deserve it,' Edie said. 'You played well. A real pro. I'll let you know the exact count when I see you next. There might be more coming your way.'

Chris stuffed the fifty pounds into his pocket. 'Just keep it coming,' he said.

16

ONE DAY AFTER work, Dave Brill took Luke Tremble for a drink. They climbed into Brill's work van – a white Toyota Hiace with tools in the back and a roof rack for ladders – and drove to a rough pub, appropriately called The Bricklayers, which Brill knew wouldn't mind their dusty clothes. He bought them both a pint and they sat at a quiet table in a corner.

Brill looked at Luke's face and wondered how anyone could be so ugly. He was a bony looking fellow with high cheekbones, but had terrible teeth, a scar down his left cheek the curved shape of a pint glass, and unattractive scruffy brown hair and beard. The beard didn't cover his cheeks properly, just grew in little clumps. It looked false, like one you might see in a bad Civil War drama on TV, and his teeth were even worse. They were brown and uneven and one of the front molars was missing, leaving a large gap whenever he smiled. Brill wondered if he ever got laid.

'When was the last time you had a woman?' he asked.

Luke was surprised by the question and blushed. He hunched over his beer, his bony nose almost in it. 'What's it to you?' he said.

'Just wondering. I was just studying your beard. You really ought to do something about it you know.'

'Like what?'

'Like shave it off. They're not fashionable any more you know. You're about twenty years out of date. Women don't like them.'

'There are loads of blokes with beards. Just look around the pub, for instance.'

Brill turned in his seat and looked around. He saw what Luke meant but he was wrong. 'They're goatee beards,' he said. 'They're fashionable but full ones aren't.'

'Looks the same to me,' Luke said defensively.

'You have to shave the sides off,' Brill said. 'Can't you see the difference?' He watched as Luke looked around.

'Can't say that I do.'

Brill decided to drop it. 'You ought to get your teeth cleaned too.'

Luke sat up in exasperation. 'What is this? Pick on Luke night?'

Brill shook his head. 'I'm just telling you for your own good. If your friends can't tell you what's wrong then who can? Obviously your mum doesn't.'

'Leave my mum out of it.'

'All it takes is a trip to the dentist – a quick whiz round with one of those electric things. Your teeth will come out sparkling. It'll do wonders for your confidence.'

'There's nothing wrong with my confidence. Anyway, what does it matter? Who the hell sees them when I'm on a roof all day?'

'You're right. No one does except me. But I just thought you'd like to know. You've been with me six months and I just thought I should tell you.'

'Is that what this little drink's about? Telling me how ugly I am?'

Brill shook his head. 'No, no, no. I wanted to ask you something else.'

'As long as it's not insulting, you can carry on.'

Brill took a sip of his drink. He thought of an old Burt Reynolds film, he couldn't remember what it was called, where Burt and a few others are canoeing down a river between some mountains in a wild part of America. They happen upon some mountain men who start scaring and threatening them, giving them a hell of a rough time. What a good film that was. Brill wished he could remember its name. He was reminded of it now because of Luke's looks, exactly like one of those scary mountain men. Shit, what a thought! But his looks could come in useful for what Brill had in mind.

'When was the last time you had a fight?' he asked.

Luke grinned and said, 'You mean a fight that I got done for, or one I got away with?'

'Any category. When was the last fight?'

Luke scratched his beard. 'A couple of weeks ago I had a minor skirmish. But I was just one of several so I don't know if that counts. A few weeks before that I had another. I beat a bloke up when he was going home from the pub. I fancied his girlfriend and wanted to show him up.'

'And did it work?'

'Na. She still went home with him.'

Brill shook his head. He had known all along that Luke wasn't very smart, and this was just confirming what a head-case he was.

'Did you watch *Who Wants To Be A Millionaire?* last night?' Luke asked.

'Saw the end of it,' Brill said.

'What I can't figure out,' Luke continued, 'is that when they phone a friend, how come that friend isn't watching TV? I mean, it's the biggest quiz show on the box and the contestant phones them for help, so that friend must know he's going to be phoned, and yet he's not watching TV. When Chris Tarrant says 'hello' it's such a big surprise to them. I can't figure it out.'

Brill wondered if Luke was joking but, after a few seconds, decided he wasn't. 'It's because the show is recorded a few hours before it goes on air. Sometimes a few days before. Therefore, the so-called friend is probably sitting at home reading the paper or making the supper.'

'I thought it was live.'

'Well, it isn't.'

Luke looked at him with disbelief but slowly it seemed to sink in. Then he nodded. 'Yeah, that would work.'

Brill glanced around the pub, wondering how he had ever come to employ such a dumbo. He looked at some of the women until Luke spoke again.

'So you missed that bloke who won £125,000?'

'Yeah.'

'What a bastard. What I would do for £125,000. What would you do with that kind of money?'

'It's not that much really. It would buy you a decent house but you wouldn't have much left over. Double that would be a nice amount.'

'I'm not being greedy. A hundred and twenty-five would do me nicely.'

Brill saw the opening he'd been looking for. 'Well, I can offer you a little extra cash.'

He watched Luke's eyes widen. 'What sort of cash?'

'Five hundred. Nice and quick.'

'What is it, a bit of building work?'

'I wouldn't call it that. It's knocking something down rather than putting something up.'

Brill saw the confused look come on Luke's face. 'I'm not following you,' he said.

Brill took another sip of beer. Luke had still barely touched his, although Brill was sure his nose had. 'I want you to damage someone for me. Someone who's got it coming.'

Luke smiled at last, revealing all those bad teeth. 'Now you're talking,' he said. Then he picked up his beer and downed it all in one go.

Brill looked at him with amazement. There was foam all around his lips and he licked it away with an enormous tongue, just like a dog. His hired hand was full of surprises and he wondered if he'd be able to keep him under control.

After another pint, Brill drove Luke to the station in the Toyota Hiace. Then he drove round to Rosetta's and let himself in. He found her lying on the sofa watching TV again, wearing white jeans and a green sweater. He felt horny straightaway and knelt down and started kissing her.

'Yuk!' she said, pushing him away. 'The smell of beer. You know how much I hate that!' So Brill went to the bathroom and brushed his teeth.

When he came back he sat down beside her and put her legs on his lap. He saw that she was watching a programme about mobile phones. She said to him, 'Did you know that in years to come there'll be a lot of one-eared people walking around?'

'What do you mean?' he said.

'Mobile phones. That's what this programme's all about. The radiation from a mobile phone can cause cancer of the ear. They should carry a health warning. In years to come, lots of people will be having their ears amputated.'

Brill sneered at her. 'Don't be silly. They wouldn't be able to sell them if that was true.'

'You're so naïve,' she said with disgust. 'One day you'll learn. You're using yours all the time.'

Brill scratched his head and watched the programme for a while. Sure enough, a few of the interviewees were having ear trouble and one of them had cancer. They named the particular make of mobile and Brill was relieved to see it wasn't the kind he used. But it was still a bit worrying. He would hate having only one ear. He unclipped his mobile from his waist and set it on the armrest.

When the programme ended, he picked up the remote and turned the TV off. Rosetta looked at him. 'So what did you have in mind, big boy?'

'For tonight?'

'Yes. Tonight.'

'Well, first I wanted to ask you something.'

'Okay.'

Brill took a deep breath. He was worried how Rosetta would respond. They had made up since the first time he had brought up the Chris Small subject and had been having great sex for the past few weeks. He wondered if he was about to put all that in jeopardy again. 'You remember that night I told you about Chris Small?'

'How could I forget?' Rosetta said.

'Well, I can't get him out of my mind and I need your help.'

'Oh yeah?'

'I want to lure him somewhere and I thought I might use you as bait.'

Rosetta let out a deep breath. 'Say that again?'

'I want to lure Chris Small somewhere and I want to use you as the bait.'

'That's exactly what I thought you said. And what will happen to him when he's lured somewhere?'

'He'll get what's coming to him, in the form of a damn good hiding.'

'And who's going to give him this hiding? You?'

'Yup,' Brill lied.

'I never had you down as a fighting man.'

'I've done my share,' Brill lied again. 'I just think he deserves it. I can't get the pitiful face of Kevin Jenkins' dad out of my mind.'

He watched Rosetta turn to the TV as if it were still on. Then she turned back to him. 'I can see this problem is never going to go away, so for just this once I'll help you. I think you're bloody mad just the same, though.'

'Maybe I am,' Brill said.

'Well at least you admit that much. Just so long as you don't kill him or anything.'

Brill had to laugh at that. 'What do you think I am? I've got far too much to lose.'

'Just so long as you realise that.'

'I do. I do.'

They fell into a silence and Brill felt triumphant. He hadn't thought it would be as easy as that.

'Well you'd better give me the details,' Rosetta said. 'I could do with some excitement at the moment. Maybe this will fill the gap.'

Brill couldn't help but smile. He patted her on the leg and said, 'Well, this is what I've got in mind.'

17

LUKE TREMBLE WAS that rarity in modern-day life: a person who commuted out of the city to get to work, rather than in to it. He lived in London, near Camden Town, on the Hampstead Road, in a twenty-storey council block called Gillhead, with his mother. He had been there for the whole of his twenty-three years; one of the many single-parent families that filled up the eighty flats.

At the age of sixteen – after leaving school with just one GCSE – Luke started working as a cleaner at Gillhead and the two other council blocks on the small Anthill Estate. Each morning, he would get up at six, dress in the council uniform of grey trousers and green sweatshirt, and start sweeping and mopping every one of the twenty floors in the Gillhead block. After that he would move outside and start collecting rubbish from the surrounding area with a spike and a black rubbish bag. Other cleaning duties followed for the rest of the day – he was part of a team of three – before he finished at four o'clock. He would then stumble into the shower, have a snooze for an hour or so, and be ready for the evening ahead.

After three years of cleaning, and deciding there was no future in it, Luke drifted into building work. He laboured on various sites in London until he came to the realisation that he couldn't stand the city any more. It was getting too crowded. People were rude, in too much of a hurry and it was time to try something different. He found building work in the suburbs until his eventual teaming up with Dave Brill.

On the train ride home, Luke thought about Dave's offer. He was basically going to pay him five hundred pounds to break one of the limbs of someone called Chris Small. Dave had a grudge against Small for something that had happened in the past – Luke had already forgotten what – and wanted him to get his comeuppance. Luke didn't mind having to break an arm or a leg – he was always looking for new experiences – and the five hundred pounds would certainly come in useful. His only outlay would be to buy a baseball bat to do the job with.

Luke's fighting habit had started in his teenage years. In the evenings, he had mixed with other single boys on the Anthill estate and they'd roamed the streets of Camden looking for trouble. He would often stay out until early morning, returning to drink beer and smoke dope in the corridors of one of the council blocks, before picking a fight with anyone he could goad. When he became a cleaner though, he became angry with other kids who littered and fought in the corridors, so he took his violent habits into the football grounds of London.

In the early days, Luke never supported a particular team, so with a gang of four or five would just turn up on a Saturday at the ground with the most trouble potential for that day – and there were fourteen London teams to choose from. Sometimes they had tickets for the game, but usually they didn't bother. On ticket-less days, they would just hang out in bars near the ground and drift into a fight after the match.

For Luke, the most exciting part of football violence was the running battles in the Underground. Fans travelling into London were always confused by the Underground system, and it was so easy to trap them, do the business, then make a quick getaway. Luke's friends nicknamed him The Mole because of his fondness for the underground skirmishes, but Luke could never see the logic, seeing as how he was over six-feet tall.

Luke also went abroad when England played, but after an incident in a Dutch bar, when a beer glass was smashed in his face, he drifted out of football and just sought the occasional fight in the many London bars he frequented at weekends. He also started supporting Arsenal, as they seemed to be the only London team that won anything.

At Charing Cross station, Luke pushed through the commuters making their way home. They annoyed him immensely as they came at him like a herd of cattle, and he had to dodge his way through. But he also found it amusing that he had beaten the rat race and they hadn't; the train he had just used was virtually empty while these poor souls would be fighting for every available seat. They might be wearing suits and earning more money, but were they any smarter?

Luke walked to Charing Cross Road and waited for a 24 or 29 bus. In theory, he could walk home – it only took twenty-five minutes – but after a long, physical day he rarely felt like it. He stood in a short queue, and when the bus arrived he jumped on.

Ten minutes later, the bus dropped him at his stop. He crossed the road, bought some milk in the twenty-four-hour garage, then walked the fifty yards to the Anthill Estate.

Apart from the three twenty-storey blocks, the estate had two children's playgrounds and a circular, tarmac play area surrounded by a high wire fence. On the play area were two basketball hoops and two undersize football goalposts. Luke had spent many summer evenings kicking a ball around but, since he'd started his building career, rarely had the energy any more. He looked across there now and saw three tiny black kids trying to throw a ball into one of the basketball hoops. He had to smile. They were so small there was no way they were going to get it in.

His mother's flat was on the fifth floor, a quick ride in the piss-smelling elevator. The flat itself had two bedrooms, with a large living room and small balcony. The balcony had wire netting around it to keep out the hundreds of pigeons that congregated on the estate. It didn't stop them from shitting all over the balcony wall though and, once a month, Luke went out with a bucket and rag and cleaned it all off.

He found his mother in the kitchen, preparing the evening meal. They said hello to each other as Luke fixed himself a cup of tea.

'Good day?' she asked half-heartedly, as she stirred something in a pot.

'Pretty good,' Luke said. 'Looks like a bit of extra work coming my way and an extra five hundred quid. We'll be able to get some carpet in here at last.'

The floor of their flat was covered entirely with grey lino, and Luke had always wanted his mother to buy some carpet – at least in the living room – so it would look like a normal flat. His mother had put it off for years though, saying she couldn't afford it, but with this five hundred pounds maybe the job would finally get done. Luke had always wanted to feel a soft carpet under his feet while watching TV.

His mother looked up and smiled. She was only twenty years older than him and still managed to find herself regular boyfriends. But Luke didn't get involved with them any more. If they pretended they wanted to be his father figure, he gave them the cold shoulder. He had been disappointed too many times to put his faith in any of them.

'You're a good boy, Luke,' she said. 'Always putting your mother first.' She was wearing tight blue jeans like she always did at home, and she had good slim legs for someone in her forties. Her hair was dyed ginger and her face was still attractive, although there were quite a few lines appearing on her forehead.

'Well, I don't need it,' Luke said. 'I don't seem to spend money any more. It would be nice to have carpet in here though.'

'It would and that's a good way to be. Better than being in debt.'

His mother had a part-time job in a Leicester Square ticket booth, selling concert and theatre tickets to tourists. She didn't make much money from it, so Luke was happy to pitch in when he could. She did, however, get a lot of cheap theatre tickets, and disappeared to shows or concerts once or twice a week. She always offered tickets to Luke, but going to the theatre wasn't high on his list of social priorities. Why would he want to sit and watch a load of poofy actors wearing make-up and talking in posh accents? He was quite happy staying indoors, watching Sky Sports.

'So what is the extra work?' his mother asked.

Luke put a tea bag into a cup and poured in some water. He didn't offer to make his mother one because she only ever drank coffee, and that was in the morning.

'Just some physical work. Knocking something down. Shouldn't take me too long, either.'

'Sounds ideal. Let me know when you've got the money and we can go and choose the carpet together.'

'Great,' Luke said.

'When would you like supper?'

'Let me have a shower and then I'll be ready.'

They always ate in silence, with the TV on, at a circular wooden table in the living room. His mother watched all the soap operas and there was always one on whenever they ate. Luke watched half-heartedly but couldn't be bothered with them. He would stare at the screen if a nice-looking woman came on, then go back to his food when it was blokes. Most days he didn't even know which show they were watching. He could only differentiate if they were wearing police or hospital uniforms.

Luke picked up the plates afterwards and took them into the kitchen. He always washed the dishes while his mother finished her soap viewing. She rarely watched TV after eight o'clock, so Luke could then go back in and watch sport, while his mother either read magazines in her bedroom or went to a show.

He spent the evening watching Spanish football; an exciting game that finished 2-1. He found he could watch almost any match these days, even if it was a dull Italian game. When the football season was over, though, he found the couple of months in-between very hard to get through. He wasn't a cricket fan so there was very little for him to do with his spare time. Those were the months when his fighting usually increased. He would go to pubs and look for trouble, just to keep his interest in life ticking over. Apart from the one jail sentence for beating up the ticket collector, he had never been charged with anything so he must be doing something right.

At eleven o'clock he went to his small bedroom, stripped off and climbed into bed. He looked at the plain magnolia walls for five minutes and felt his eyes starting to droop. He never had trouble sleeping after a hard day's work. He reached over and turned off the bedside light.

18

'SO THIS IS where you live?'

Brad walked into Chris's room and looked around.

'I'm afraid so,' Chris said.

'Is it cheap?'

'Three hundred a month.'

'Not so cheap.'

'No. But in Elmhurst there's not much available. I had to take what I could get.'

Brad looked puzzled for a second. 'No TV? No hi-fi?'

'I had them nicked,' Chris said. 'The day before I met Edie, in fact.'

'Oh yeah. I remember her telling me.'

'That's one reason why I'm on board. So I can make some money to buy replacements.'

'Well that shouldn't be any problem.'

'Hopefully not. But I'm not feeling too confident after our last outing.'

Chris made them both a cup of tea and they sat at the small metal table by the window. It was Sunday afternoon and they were going to practise a few signaling moves because, on their second casino outing, they had lost over two hundred pounds. Edie would be turning up later to chip in with her ideas.

Chris and Brad played for an hour, smoothing out things that had gone wrong. The trouble with card counting was that it was still no guarantee of success. If some good cards were meant to come your way at a particular moment, then the dealer was just as likely to get them as you. Chris sometimes found it all a bit demoralising. After an hour of practising, he needed a break.

'So what's your opinion of Edie's gambling?' he asked. 'Are

you waiting for the day when she'll stop or doesn't it bother you?'

'It doesn't bother me at the moment,' Brad said. 'She's pretty disciplined and wins most of the time. I'm not sure if I'd like to put up with it over a number of years, though.'

'Isn't it something you should talk about before you get married?'

'We have talked about it. She reckons she'll quit.'

'And you believe her?'

'Yeah. Maybe.' Brad nodded, unconvincingly.

Chris looked out of the window at the street below. People were walking their dogs around the pond on the opposite side of the road, which was about as exciting as things got in Elmhurst.

'What's with the Plasticine around your windows?' Brad asked.

'It keeps out the draught,' Chris said. 'I peel it off in the summer, put it back in the winter.'

'The windows look a bit rotten. You've got damp on that wall as well.' He pointed at the sloping part of the ceiling, behind where Chris was sitting.

'Tell me about it. It gets dripping wet when I've got the heater on. But that's just one of the regular things you put up with in rented accommodation. One room I had a long time ago, the bed was right next to a damp wall. I would wake up in the morning with damp sheets. In the end I came down with pleurisy.'

'With all due respect,' Brad said, 'I couldn't live in a place like this.' He turned in his chair. 'I mean, look at this heater. It's barbaric!'

'I wouldn't go that far. Actually, it keeps the room very warm. I know it's not The Ritz but, as I said before, I've seen worse.' Chris didn't like it when people made judgements on the places he lived. He lived in places he could afford. Brad was a middle-class American. His parents were probably comfortably off and he'd probably never lived anywhere rough. He decided to change the subject. 'So why do people gamble?' he asked.

Brad turned back round. 'A variety of reasons. Mostly because they're lazy and want to get rich quickly. They think gambling will do it for them. Then when they lose, they start to chase their bets and get into a real mess. Others do it for the thrill of getting that big win. The thrill will outweigh all their losses and they'll go for it again. They, too, will end up in debt.'

'You're not making me feel too hopeful.'

'Then you have the third type: the minority that actually knows what they're doing. They read books, study the form. They also have a mathematical brain. Those minorities are the ones that win. And some of them are very good.'

'And does Edie fall into that category?'

'She's good. She has to work at it, though. And I'm not sure she has that great mathematical brain that the really good gamblers have. But she's got persistence and common sense. She's got good money-management, knows how to look after her bankroll. She's better than most.'

'Well, I'm relieved to hear that.'

'Just because we had one loss, I wouldn't worry too much. We'll get that back.'

Chris looked at his watch. It was after three o'clock. 'So, these smart gamblers, the ones with the mathematical brains. What games do they tend to specialise in?'

'In a casino?'

'Yeah.'

'It'll be games like blackjack, poker or baccarat. It's a long slog making money at blackjack, so poker is what most of them concentrate on. In poker, you're not up against the casino, you're playing against other players, so you have more chance of making money. It's also more sociable. You can chat to the other players and have a laugh. You can't really do that with blackjack. The game to avoid is roulette. There are plenty of fools around who think they can make money from it, but they really need their heads examining. They come up with all sorts of systems to beat it but they're all bullshit. They're living in a dream world.'

'What about something like horse racing?'

'Some people make a living at it, but there's a lot of hard work involved. Studying form, getting to know the horses, trainers and jockeys. Sports betting is very big in the States and it's catching on over here now. Loads of betting on football matches and games like golf and tennis. For the lonely and isolated there's gambling on the Internet, better know as 'nambling'. It's a bit too risky, though. Far too many things can go wrong and loads of crooks are involved, apparently.'

'Nambling?'

'Net gambling.'

'Oh, yeah.'

'Have you heard of spread betting?'

'No.'

'Well that's catching on over here as well. It's going to be very big. You bet on a spread of scores rather than specific scores. You have an account with the bookies and you can change your prediction while a game is being played. People also spread bet on the stock market. There are quite a few smart city people making good money at it.'

'I think that's way beyond me.'

'Me too. You have to be very money-minded, very focused.'

'So how come you know so much about gambling?'

'I've read a bit about it. There are lots of good stories around and some great characters. I used to be into it more when I was card counting. I more or less paid my way through college by playing blackjack. You wouldn't think it to look at my playing now.' Brad laughed.

'You seem pretty good to me. Especially your acting talents.'

Brad laughed again. 'I read recently about this crazy gambler who does wild things for money? A friend of his bet him $100,000 that he wouldn't dare to have breast implants and keep them in for a year.'

'You're joking!'

'It's true. So he got the implants and kept them in for a year. And the other guy paid up.'

'Jesus. I wouldn't want to have breasts for a year.'

'The funny thing is, he said women couldn't get enough of him. They were queuing up to go to bed with him, so from that point of view it was well worth it.'

'What kind of a woman would want a man with breasts?'

'Bisexual ones.'

'Bisexual ones?'

'Think about it.'

Chris thought about it and said, 'The best-of-both-worlds syndrome?'

'That's right. In fact, this guy kept them in for longer than a year and, for all I know, he's still got them. He's having too good a time to get rid of them.'

Chris thought he'd heard everything now. He shook his head. 'I don't think it'll catch on,' he said.

He got up to make some more tea but then heard his front doorbell ring. He went downstairs and found Edie on the doorstep. He kissed her on the lips as she came in, their usual greeting now, even when Brad was around. He still found her incredibly sexy, even though he knew nothing would ever come of their relationship.

'Did you find it all right?' he asked.

'Your directions were perfect,' she said. 'Have you boys been having a good time?'

'Yeah. Ironing out all the problems and talking about breast implants. Follow me.'

He led her upstairs and looked at her reaction to his room. She didn't seem to mind it at all. He made them all a cup of tea then sat on the bed while the other two took the chairs. They made small talk for a while then Edie came out with what was on her mind.

'The thing is, Chris,' she said, 'we really need you to chip in on the stake. We can't just play with my bankroll all the time.

It's too small. If we carry on with our present betting routine, it'll take ages getting anywhere. We need to up our bets. Brad's agreed to chip in five hundred. How much can you come up with?'

Chris felt alarm bells ringing in his head. He still had the thousand pounds in the building society he hadn't told them about. 'Will we win more with a bigger bankroll?' he asked.

Edie nodded. 'It means we can hit harder at the appropriate times. Our winnings will be bigger.'

'But our losses could be bigger as well?'

'That's a possibility. There will always be upturns and downturns. But we need more money behind us to do well. I feel as if I'm restricted at the moment.'

They all fell into a silence. Chris felt as if the eyes of the world were on him. If he wanted to break up the threesome he would have to do it now. But did he really want to? He had become quite attached to these two and wanted to keep their company for a while longer. He wanted to see how it all panned out and it was obviously going to cost him a bit of his savings. But then again, he might end up with more.

'If Brad's putting in five hundred then I'll do the same,' he said. Edie and Brad both smiled. 'How much does that take our bankroll up to?'

'Nearly two and a half thousand,' Edie said. 'That's much more like it.'

With the deal done they did a bit more practising and then it was time for Edie and Brad to go. They arranged their next meeting for Wednesday, then Chris walked them down to the front door.

'You won't regret it,' Brad said. 'Now we'll really make those casinos squirm.'

Chris hoped he was right. He kissed Edie and shook Brad's hand.

He stood at the top of the stone steps outside and watched them walk down. Then he waved as they disappeared from sight.

Glancing at the car park of the pub across the road, Chris noticed two people sitting in a black BMW, looking right at him. He looked right back at them and then went indoors.

19

DAVE BRILL SHUDDERED when Chris Small looked at him, and wondered if he'd been recognised. When Small went back inside, he looked at Rosetta. 'What do you think?'

Rosetta smiled. 'He's good-looking. He doesn't look like the tough guy you said he was.'

Brill felt a pang of jealousy. He didn't like Rosetta thinking Small was good-looking. 'He's not a tough guy, he's a manipulator. He gets people doing things and then they end up dead.'

Rosetta looked at him, her eyes in shadow from a large, dark blue hat she was wearing. 'Manipulator? Excuse me, but isn't that exactly what you're doing at the moment? Trying to manipulate me into helping you?'

Brill paused for a few seconds. He hadn't thought of it that way. 'Maybe. But I'm doing it for a good purpose.'

'Which is?'

'Giving him some payback for wrongdoings. Setting the world to rights.'

Rosetta shook her head. 'You men. You're all the same. Playing your little games. Not caring who gets hurt. You should've been a politician. Then you could have started a war and had some serious fun.'

Brill fell into a sulk. He felt like telling Rosetta to get lost. He hated it when she talked to him like that; like she was telling off a little boy. Just because she was older than him, did that mean she was any wiser? 'So are you in?' he forced himself to say.

'Oh, I'm in all right,' she said. 'It'll be interesting to see what a fool you make of yourself.'

Brill smiled to himself. He'd got what he wanted for now. He started the BMW and drove slowly out of the car park.

When they were moving along the road, he started to relax. Driving his prized possession always made him feel much better. 'Fancy a drink somewhere?' he asked.

'If you're buying.'

'There's a new All Bar One in Bromley. I went in there the other day and it's pretty good.'

'I didn't have you down as an All Bar One man.'

'I'm full of surprises,' Brill said. 'It can be our new meeting place.'

When Chris got back upstairs he was feeling a little on edge. He was pretty sure the man downstairs, in the BMW, was the builder who'd knocked on his door a couple of weeks ago. He wasn't a hundred per cent sure, but he had pretty good eyesight, even in the fading light. And he'd had someone with him as well, a woman, although he couldn't make out her face because she'd been wearing a large hat. He added it to the list of his other present concerns.

He was also worried about Hugh, his Sunday worker at the off-licence. One of his regulars had come into the shop during the week and told him that, when he'd bought some booze the Sunday before, Hugh hadn't rung the amount into the till. The customer was a security guard for Marks & Spencer in Oxford Street and such behaviour had immediately seemed suspicious to him. It seemed suspicious to Chris as well. If Hugh wasn't ringing a sale into the till it could only mean one thing: he was pocketing the money. The security guard – Chris didn't know his name – had promised to go in and buy something today and let Chris know the score next week. If Hugh was pocketing money, that meant Chris would have to give him the sack, and that would mean going back to his six-day week until he found another employee. What a drag that would be. But if Hugh was nicking money, he would have to go. Chris didn't like being taken for a ride, even if the off-licence wasn't his business.

His third concern was the five hundred pounds he had just

promised to Edie and Brad. Tomorrow, he would go to the building society and draw it out. It was only the money he had illegally obtained in Boroughheath, the money Amanda had given back to him, but he still hated to part with it. He would have to hope that the investment would be a good one and he would build on it over the long term.

As today was the last of the week, and he had only had two drinking days so far, he decided to crack open a bottle of wine. He spent the rest of the evening playing blackjack on his computer, and found that the drunker he got, the more he lost. He wasn't too surprised at this revelation and fell into bed at ten o'clock, feeling more relaxed than he had a few hours earlier.

The next day he woke up late, with a hangover. He climbed out of bed and put on his dressing gown and slippers.

Monday was his favourite day of the week because, being his day off, he had the whole house to himself. He headed for the bathroom for a long soak but first had to wash the bath, which always had a black ring around the side.

He climbed out half an hour later and had a shave. He dried himself and went back upstairs.

He still had a slight headache after he was dressed. How many times had he told himself not to drink the evening before his day off, because it invariably ruined it? And how many times had he just gone straight ahead and done it anyway?

As he was putting on his shoes the gas fire flickered out. He swore out loud. He would have to go and get a full bottle, another hassle he could do without. He would do it first and get it over with.

He unscrewed the bottle from the portable fire, put on his coat and carried the bottle downstairs to the front door. His means of transport was sitting by the kitchen entrance: a former mobile shopping basket that was now just a metal frame on wheels, with two straps. He lifted the bottle on to it and tied up the two straps. Carrying an empty bottle wasn't any problem but there was no way he could carry a full one back. Therefore, the frame on wheels was essential.

After opening the front door, Chris carried the whole contraption down the stone steps. He set it on the pavement and started wheeling it towards the main street. This was one of the most demeaning things he had ever had to do in his life, and each time it happened he swore it would be the last.

There was a zebra crossing on the main road that led to Elmhurst Pond on the other side. The traffic stopped to let him cross and he wondered what the motorists were thinking. Then he trundled along past mothers with prams; his own little pram wobbling behind him, his iron baby much quieter than theirs. They looked at him as if he were mad.

On the other side of the pond he turned left and then it was just a fifty-yard walk to the hardware shop. He crossed another zebra crossing and walked in the front door.

'Another one of these, please,' he said to the shop assistant, who looked at the orange gas bottle as if he'd never seen one before.

'Haven't got any,' he said, shaking his head slowly.

Chris couldn't believe what he was hearing. 'What do you mean, you haven't got any?'

'Didn't get our delivery last week. It's coming on Wednesday I think.' Then he was glancing at the front door as a woman entered.

Chris felt like screaming. It meant he would have to wheel the bottle all the way home and go without gas until next Monday, when he would have to do it all again, unless he got up very early on Thursday. He would ring next time to make sure they had some. But he didn't have a telephone. He would have to use a payphone. Everything just got more complicated.

'Maybe I could help.'

Chris turned, not sure if he was being spoken to or not. He swivelled the basket round in the direction of the door. He could feel his face dripping sweat, partly from pulling the trolley, partly from anger.

'Maybe I could help,' the voice said again, and Chris was surprised to find the woman who had just entered looking directly at him. She nodded at his empty bottle. 'I have a car,' she said. 'My local hardware shop sells those. It's over in Sidcup. I'll give you a lift, if you like.'

'No, it's all right,' Chris said.

'It isn't any problem,' the woman smiled.

'Are you sure? I don't want to put you to any trouble.'

'It's no trouble at all,' the woman said. 'I'm just about to go there anyway. Then I'll run you back, if you like.'

Chris couldn't believe this was happening. Never before in his life had a complete stranger offered to go out of their way to help him. And a good-looking woman as well.

'Well, okay,' he said. 'That would be great.' He nodded at the shop assistant, who now had a look of envy on his face.

They walked around the corner to where her car was parked, Chris pulling on the shopping basket. She opened the boot and he lifted the whole thing inside. 'I hope you realise I didn't invent this,' he joked.

The woman laughed and said, 'I would hope not.'

They climbed inside her car and headed towards Sidcup.

'So what brings you to Elmhurst?' Chris asked.

'Just a change,' the woman said. 'It's a nice little village. It has some interesting shops. Sidcup isn't very exciting.'

They made more small talk about the local area. Chris was able to look the woman over as she drove. He put her in her late forties, with long, shapely legs, dyed-blonde hair, and a good strong face. She was wearing black leggings and a brown jacket and he thought she was very attractive for her age.

When they arrived in Sidcup, the woman drove down the high street, then down a side street and pulled over. 'Here it is,' she said. 'Let's see if they've got any.'

They walked into the hardware shop, confirmed they had some gas, then went back to the car for the bottle. They exchanged it for a full one, put it in the boot, then drove back to Elmhurst.

When they were parked outside Chris's lodgings, he invited the woman in for a cup of tea. She hesitated for a second or two and then said 'Okay.'

He took the gas bottle out of the boot and watched while she parked in the pub car park. Then she walked back towards him, Chris watching her long legs moving nicely. They walked up the stone steps, Chris carrying the now quite heavy gas bottle. He dumped it by the door and reached in his pocket for keys.

When the woman was beside him, he said, 'My name's Chris, by the way.' He put out his hand to shake hers.

'And mine's Rosetta,' she said.

20

ROSETTA DIDN'T KNOW what to make of Chris Small's lodgings; it had been so many years since she'd been in a rented room. She was used to people with their own houses, and she supposed that was a sign of her age and middle-class status. After all, there was no way she would date a man who rented a room, so why would she ever be in one? And this one merely confirmed her theory. There was paint peeling off the sloping ceiling and Plasticine stuck in gaps in the windows. And there was no TV, no CD player: just a laptop computer sitting on the floor.

She watched Small while he made a cup of tea. Short brown hair, nice face, and a good body. He looked younger than Dave, probably in his late twenties or early thirties. It would be quite an achievement if she got him into bed. And why shouldn't she? Dave had told her to get to know him, lure him into a trap, and if she could have some fun along the way then why not? After all, Dave was beginning to bore her. He was such an overweight slob, and maybe it was time to move on.

They sat opposite each other on uncomfortable metal chairs, leaning on a white metal table, looking down on the high street. Rosetta could tell that Small liked her by the way he was looking at her, the way he was turning on the charm. It went through her mind to jump into bed with him right now, but she didn't think she could do it in such a lumpy looking bed in such an unattractive room. She would have to invite him round to her house, but how could she do that in a subtle way? And she would have to do it without Dave knowing.

She decided to pry into Small's past. They were talking about his present job so she innocently asked, 'Have you always worked in off-licences?'

'No,' he said. 'But I wouldn't want to bore you with all the others. I've had too many jobs to mention.'

'Where was the first off-licence?'

'In Boroughheath.'

Rosetta feigned surprise. 'I know Boroughheath well. Was it the one in the high street?'

She saw a look of suspicion come into Small's eyes. 'Yeah. Just near the shopping centre.'

'And how long were you there for?'

'About a year and a half.'

'You may have served me. I used to shop there sometimes.'

'Now that would be a major coincidence.'

'It's a small world. So why did you leave there?'

Now Small was looking at her very strangely. 'I hated the area. I also didn't like my boss. He was a lazy sod. I've spent most of my life wondering how most of my bosses got to where they are. Have you found that?'

Now he was switching the conversation back to her. She decided to back off from her line of questioning. 'I've been a kept woman for the last ten years, I'm afraid. Before that, I was a housewife. I haven't had a job since my mid-twenties. Do you think that's bad?'

'Not necessarily. It depends what you want to do with your life. I mean, I've worked my whole life since I was sixteen and still have nothing to show for it. At least you have your own house. I have this.' He waved his arm at the room.

Rosetta felt a little sorry for him. 'You'll have to come and see my house,' she said. 'I'll fix you a meal sometime.'

'That would be nice,' Small said, and she could see a wicked glint in his eye.

She picked up a pen from the table and wrote her telephone number down on a pad that was lying there. 'Here's my number. Give me a ring any time. I'm always in.'

'Okay.'

'I'd better be going.'

'Are you sure?'

'I just realised I never did buy what I went into the hardware shop for. You distracted me.' Rosetta was impressed with her lie and surprised at how easy it came. She watched a smile come on Chris Small's face.

'Sorry,' he shrugged.

'The pleasure was all mine,' she teased.

They stood up and he walked her downstairs. Rosetta made sure she went first so Small could have a nice long look at her backside. She'd often been told she had a great arse and she knew it looked good in her black leggings.

At the front door, they shook hands and she gave him a nice smile. 'Give me a ring sometime,' she said.

'I will,' Small said.

Then she turned and went down the stone steps. She felt better about herself than she had for a long time.

Chris stood on the doorstep and watched Rosetta walk back to her car in the pub car park. Such a nice figure, and a nice woman too. When she reached her car she turned and waved. He would leave it a few days and then give her a ring. Who knew where it might lead?

He went back upstairs then realised he still had to go to the building society to get out the five hundred pounds. He picked up his savings book and jacket and went back outside.

There was only one building society in Elmhurst and it wasn't the one Chris used, so he had to walk up to the main road and wait for a bus to Bromley. It took ten minutes for one to appear and in another ten minutes he was walking along Bromley High Street.

He was feeling in good spirits after his meeting with Rosetta and didn't even feel too bad as he handed his savings book over for the withdrawal. He asked for ten fifty-pound notes and put them in his wallet before leaving.

Over the years, Chris had shopped many times in Bromley and liked walking around their indoor shopping centre, probably the only indoor centre he could stomach. He spent an hour looking at clothes and CDs, and even stopped in some of the gift shops. It was tempting to buy something with all the money he had on him but he restrained himself and walked out empty-handed.

Back on the high street he felt a little hungry and fancied getting a late lunch and a drink. He wondered where to go and started walking along until he saw a new All Bar One he had never been in. He checked to make sure they did food and then stepped inside.

He saw Rosetta almost as soon as he'd entered, sitting at a back table with a man; a man Chris recognised to be the builder who had tried getting into his home. The shock of seeing them together froze him in mid-step, until he realised he'd better get out of sight. He did a complete U-turn and walked straight back outside.

He stood on the doorstep, a cold sweat appearing on his forehead. He felt totally confused. What the hell was going on? Why was Rosetta sitting with that bloke? The only reason he could come up with was that they must know each other, and that they were up to no good. He kicked the wall in anger and then walked off.

At the bus stop he stood in a short queue, his head still reeling. He felt more than a little disappointed that his meeting with Rosetta was obviously a set-up. She had followed him to the hardware store and intentionally made contact. She was obviously in cahoots with the builder – but why?

When the bus came along, Chris found a seat by the window and looked out in a daze. His stomach was churning and it was starting to rain. To add to his problems, he was now going to get wet when he walked back to his room.

For the rest of the afternoon, he tried thinking of a reasonable answer but couldn't. He sat stone-cold sober in his room, in front of the gas fire, staring at Rosetta's phone number on the pad of paper. Eventually, he tore it up and threw it in the bin.

He spent the evening practising blackjack on his computer

again and started to relax. Once again, solving logical problems took his mind off problems with no solution. Maybe he should just cut people off completely and play computer games. Sometimes that seemed a much safer thing to do.

21

'THIS HOUSE LOOKS like a disaster area to me,' Luke said, looking up the side wall of their latest job and shaking his head.

'I agree,' Brill said. 'You can see how the damp from the chimneys has spread down the walls. Look at the colour of the bricks. They're a lot darker than the dry ones.'

'And flaky, too.'

Brill nodded. 'It's amazing the money people will spend on these old dumps. I blame it all on *Changing Rooms*.'

Luke looked at him with a baffled expression. 'What do you mean?'

'I mean, they buy dilapidated buildings so they can rip them apart and practise their DIY skills. It's been called the *Changing Rooms* syndrome.'

'Why's that?'

'Don't you ever watch *Changing Rooms*?'

'Can't say that I do.'

Brill wondered whether it was worth the energy explaining. He decided to keep it simple. 'It's a programme about doing DIY on your house. It's the biggest DIY programme on TV. Everyone watches it. Everyone except you, it seems.'

Luke shrugged. 'Yeah well. I've got a life. I don't have time to watch such things.'

'So you've never heard of Carol Smillie either?'

'Carol who?'

Brill decided to drop it. What was the point in even trying?

'So you think our job will fix it?' Luke asked.

'I doubt it. But if that's what they want, then that's what they'll get.'

Brill had been in the house a month ago, looking at the damage inside, before sending the young couple a quote. Both the bedrooms had large damp patches where the chimneys met the ceilings. When they'd bought the house, three layers of wallpaper had covered the damp. The couple hadn't discovered it until they'd started their DIY, changing their rooms. The situation was too big for their modest skills so they'd given Brill a ring. He almost felt sorry for people who had such serious structural problems but reckoned it was their fault for buying such an old property in the first place. There was no way he would buy a house as old as this.

He had been asked to fix up the chimneys, which were slowly crumbling away. He would have to rebuild half of them, and then put on new rendering and cowlings on top. And he would bet his life it still wouldn't fix the damp problem. There was some deeper problem about this house that maybe only a complete new roof would solve. But that wasn't his worry. He had agreed to do the work as specified and it would earn him just over one-and-a-half thousand pounds. And it should only take three or four days.

'I saw Rosetta yesterday,' he said, still looking up at the walls. It was seven-thirty in the morning and the first job would be to put up a scaffolding tower.

'And?' Luke said.

'She made contact with our target and reckons she can set him up pretty soon. She's going to aim for a weekend, a Sunday, because he works Saturdays. How would that be for you?'

'Fine.'

'You'll have to catch the train to Sidcup and I can pick you up. I'll drive you to her house and then we can do him.'

Luke looked at him for the first time. 'What do you mean, we? I thought I was going to do it on my own.'

'You are, but I want to be there to see it. Otherwise, where's the satisfaction for me? I've got to see him get his pain.'

Luke nodded. 'Okay. If that's the way you want it.' He looked back up at the chimneys. 'It won't be this weekend, will it?'

Brill shook his head. 'No. Probably the one after. Why?'

Luke looked at him again. 'Arsenal are live on Sky. I wouldn't want to miss that.'

Chris had only been at work a few hours on Tuesday when the security guard from Marks & Spencer came in. He had a serious look on his face as he came over to the till.

'He was at it again,' he said.

Chris nodded. 'Tell me the bad news.'

The security guard leaned on the counter. He was a stocky man, with the air of superiority that all security guards seemed to have. But Chris didn't mind that at all, as long as he was supplying him with useful information. 'I bought a bottle of Chilean red for four ninety-nine and gave him a ten-pound note. He didn't ring it in just gave me the change. He had the till drawer open permanently. I saw him do it to someone else, as well.'

'Shit!' Chris said.

'Can't get the staff these days can you?' the guard said, in a superior tone.

'It's my fault, I shouldn't have left him alone. I didn't check him out properly. I was too eager to get Sundays off.'

'It's not your fault. You could've been with him and he still could have done it. Whenever you popped out or went to the bog. It's the oldest trick in the book.'

'I suppose so, but I still should have checked him over. In fact, I'll do that now.'

'You know where he worked before?'

'Hamleys in Covent Garden.'

Chris jumped off his stool and fetched a Yellow Pages. He rang Hamleys and asked for the manager. They chatted a few minutes and then Chris hung up. 'He was sacked for nicking money from the till.'

The security man nodded. 'There you go.'

'I can't believe it. What an idiot I've been. I hate being taken for a ride.'

'Well, it happens to us all. You'd better take references next time.'

'I will. But as I told my boss, anyone can fake references.'

'That's right.'

'I guess my judgement of character is slipping. Maybe I'm getting too soft.'

'Don't be hard on yourself. We all get conned from time to time.'

Chris nodded. 'I suppose so. Why don't you take a couple of bottles for yourself on the house. You've saved me a lot of money in the long run.'

'That's okay. It's always a pleasure to catch a thief.'

They shook hands and the man left.

Chris sulked at the till for a few minutes. He would have to come in on Sunday and relieve Hugh of his keys, and then give him the sack. He couldn't do it over the phone because then he would never see the keys again, and that would be even worse. Then he would have to stay in the shop and work. What a drag. He had just been getting used to his Sunday lie-ins.

He opened up the sales book and checked it. The figures for Sundays looked pretty normal for the past five weeks. Hugh could've taken a hundred or so each day without it being noticed. Sales could vary anywhere between four hundred and nine hundred. What a conniving little bastard. Well, he would get his comeuppance on Sunday.

Chris spent the rest of the day in a bad mood. He tried taking his mind off things by thinking about tomorrow night's gambling. He would have calmed down by then and, hopefully, they'd have a good evening.

When he got home that evening, Chris cooked a quick supper in the kitchen and carried it upstairs. He was halfway through a pork chop when his doorbell rang. He swore out loud, put on his slippers, and made the long trip back downstairs.

He wondered who it would be this time. Usually it was just people pushing the wrong bell or Jehovah's witnesses. The last time it had rung, though, had been when that builder had tried getting in. When he reached the corridor he poked his head around the corner and saw a shock of blonde hair through the mottled door glass, standing underneath the outside light. He knew it was Rosetta, no doubt about it, and dodged back out of sight.

'Hiding from someone?'

The voice made Chris jump and he turned to see Heavy Metal coming out of his room.

'There's a vamp on the doorstep who's after my body,' Chris said. 'I think I'll just let her go away.'

Squinting his eyes at the door, Heavy Metal said, 'I'll tell her to go away if you like.'

'Just ask what she wants. Tell her I'm not in.'

'Will do.'

Chris sat on the stairs and listened to the door open and then the two of them talking. Then the door closed and footsteps came back towards him.

'She's written you a note,' Heavy Metal said. He handed over an envelope with some untidy writing on it.

'Thanks,' Chris said. He had to stare at the note a while before making out that it said 'How would you like Sunday lunch at my place? Give me a ring.' And then her phone number once again.

'I told you she was after me,' Chris said. 'Wants me to have Sunday lunch with her.'

'You should take her up on it. She's a bit of a looker.'

'She's also up to something, though. And I haven't figured out what, yet.'

Heavy Metal stood looking down at him but the conversation had dried up. Chris couldn't help but look at the lump on his cheek.

'Well, I'll leave you to it,' Heavy Metal said, and then went back to his room.

'Yeah, thanks,' Chris said, and sat looking at the note a while longer.

22

THE NEXT EVENING Chris met Edie and Brad on Oxford Street and they caught a bus to The Albert casino in Edgware Road. As usual, they all went in at different times and then Chris and Brad waited for Edie to settle at a table. Chris had a Coke while he waited at the bar, and stared at the other punters.

His bad mood of yesterday still hadn't dissipated and he wondered if he was in the right frame of mind to gamble. The casinos were blurring into one and their general seediness wasn't exactly uplifting. The clientele looked seedy too, and he was sure he could never become friendly with any of them. He was more convinced than ever that gambling was a pastime for losers.

He watched Edie from a safe distance, waiting for the signal for Brad to join her. Eventually, she clasped her hands behind her head and he smiled as Brad sauntered over in his impersonation of a drunk. Then, Chris ambled over and sat down beside him.

They played quietly for ten minutes or so, Chris feeling more on edge than usual, not only because of his bad mood, but also because earlier he had handed over his five hundred pounds. Now it was like they were playing with his money as well, although of course it was only part of the larger pot. He nervously watched Brad putting on the big-player act for the benefit of the floor managers and pit bosses.

As he played, Chris watched Edie's left hand for the signal they should increase their bets. One finger tucked in to increase; two fingers to double their usual bet; three fingers to treble it; and a clenched fist to really go for it. They had had the clenched fist for the first time last week and that had been the time they had lost heavily. Chris wasn't really sure if he wanted to see the fist again.

They stayed at the table for an hour, with a variety of bets going down. Chris was starting to get bored. He won a few big hands, then lost them all back again, managing to stay even through most of it. Next to him, Brad seemed to be doing quite well, his stack of chips growing steadily as his drunken act got louder and louder. Some of the other players laughed along with him, while some, like Edie, just ignored him.

Chris didn't know how Edie could concentrate for so long. He noticed she was also scrutinising the dealers as they changed; probably looking for ones she recognised, or ones who'd brought her good luck in the past. She was also looking to see how far they penetrated the deck with the cutcard when it was time for a new deal. This was another important detail Chris was learning about. Apparently, the deeper the penetration of the six decks, the more advantageous it was for the counter. All these little things had to be looked at and taken into account. After one shallow penetration, Edie stood up, rubbed her eyes and quietly left. That meant Chris had to carry on playing Basic for a while, until he too could leave. He waited for Brad to go first and then stayed another twenty minutes.

Playing on his own, Chris soon got a lucky run of cards. He counted eight winning hands in a row and he could do no wrong as he split pairs, doubled down, and played with a confidence he had only experienced before on his computer. Maybe this gambling lark wasn't such a bad thing after all! All of a sudden, his bad mood had vanished. Playing only five pounds per hand, he was soon over sixty pounds ahead. He decided to quit and went to cash in his chips.

He picked up his coat and went to meet the others in a Burger King down the road. As he walked in, he clenched his fist as if he'd just scored a goal.

'You look pleased with yourself,' Edie said as he sat down.

'I just won sixty quid while you were away. Eight hands in

a row. Everything I did came off. Now I see how you can get hooked on this.'

'That's good going,' Brad said. 'You know you get to keep that for yourself.'

'I do?'

'Yeah. Anything you win on your own, you keep for yourself. It's only the team winnings that go into the pot.'

'Are you sure? I feel a bit guilty about keeping it. Especially when Edie's doing all the hard work.'

'Keep it,' Edie said. 'We did okay tonight and there's still another casino to go to.'

'We're going to another one?'

'May as well,' Brad said. 'The night's young and it seems as if our luck's in.'

'Let me get a burger first,' Chris said, and went up to the counter.

He had to eat his burger on the move, as Edie was so keen to get to the next casino. They caught a tube to Baker Street, to a small casino called The Piranha. The name didn't fill Chris with confidence, but once again he found himself going through the same routine: sitting down for an hour and playing quietly with the noisy Brad next to him, then playing alone when they had both gone.

He was out of there by ten-thirty and met them in a bus shelter, sitting quietly together, sheltering from a light drizzle. They both looked tired and were yawning.

They caught the tube back to Charing Cross, then sat together on the Orpington train, Chris feeling whacked by the long day. The train was full, hardly a spare seat to be found; the only sound being the occasional mobile phone ringing. Chris leant forward and asked quietly, 'How much do you think we made tonight?'

Edie and Brad looked at each other. 'Over two hundred,' Edie said. 'Wouldn't you?'

Brad nodded. 'About that. We'll add it up when we get home.'

Chris sat back in his seat and looked at them. 'Is that all? I thought we might have made more.'

'I don't think so,' Brad said.

'I thought our bigger bets would have more effect.'

Edie held a finger to her lips. She obviously didn't like Chris talking about it with other people around. 'It's all right for a beginning. We may have to go even higher, though. Nasty weather we've been having.' She smiled at Chris and he got the message.

'Nasty for this time of year,' he smiled back.

With the two hundred pounds lost last week, Chris knew they weren't that much ahead after three evenings as a team.

'Can you start making a balance sheet?' he asked, in a quiet voice. Edie and Brad looked at him strangely. 'So I know exactly how much we're going up and down. If we don't make serious headway, I may drop out. It seems a lot of work for not much return.'

'You're only saying that because you're tired,' Edie said.

'I am tired,' Chris agreed.

'What about that sixty quid you won?' Brad said. 'You thought it was all good fun then.'

Chris looked at them sheepishly. 'I gave most of it back to The Piranha after you'd both gone. I think I'm up fifteen quid for the night.'

'Well, your cut from the team's takings will make up for that,' Edie said. 'We'll start doing a balance sheet and give you one each time we meet. Brad's already been keeping a record anyway, but you should know exactly what's going on.'

'Thanks,' Chris yawned. He leant back and shut his eyes. He hadn't had any alcohol for the whole evening but still felt tired. And he still had the eighteen-minute walk home, up the steep hill. How he hated that walk on late evenings such as this.

After thirty minutes, the train pulled into Elmhurst and he said goodbye and stepped off. When he walked out of the station, he saw one taxi sitting by the rank and wondered whether he should treat himself. Then two girls got there before him and he resigned himself to the long walk.

23

SITTING IN THE locked bathroom at home, Dave Brill got out his mobile phone and rang Rosetta. It was Friday afternoon.

'Any luck?' he asked, as soon as she'd answered.

'No,' she replied. 'No luck at all. I dropped another note through his door but no bite. Maybe he just doesn't like me.'

'But you were pretty sure he did.'

'I'm a pretty good judge of these things and I was sure he did, but obviously I was wrong.'

'Maybe you should go round wearing something sexy. What were you wearing when you met him?'

'Just leggings and a jacket.'

'So he saw your shapely legs. How could he refuse? What are you wearing now?'

'I've just had a bath so I'm only wearing a towel.'

'I wish I could be there to share it with you.'

'And what's your excuse this evening?'

'Got some friends coming round. Have to stay in and play the host.'

'So you do have friends?'

'Very funny.' Brill thought for a moment. 'Maybe you could go round there one more time and wear something really sexy, like something see-through. How would that be?'

'What do you think I am? A tart or something?'

'Just thinking out loud. We have to find some way of luring him to your place. Wear something that'll make him think he's on a sure thing. No man would turn that down.'

The line went quiet for a while. Brill could imagine Rosetta sitting there in her towel, thinking about it. Although he had feelings of jealousy, he would like to see her wearing something sexy too, trying to get another man into bed. He wondered if she'd ever slept with two men before. He wouldn't put it past her.

'Hello?' he said.

'I'll give it one more go tonight,' she said. 'Of course, it would be a lot easier if he had a phone. Can you believe there isn't a phone in the whole house? He told me that the other day.'

'Unbelievable. Someone must have a mobile, though.'

'Well he certainly hasn't. Why don't these people get in the real world?'

'Beats me.' There was a knock on the bathroom door. 'Who is it?' Brill asked.

'It's someone else.' It was Tony, his four-year-old.

Brill chuckled. Someone else! He'd have to remember that one. 'I've got to go,' he said to Rosetta. 'Duty calls. Good luck tonight. I'll ring you later.'

He hung up and opened the bathroom door, but Tony had disappeared.

Rosetta got dressed slowly, savouring the thought of turning up at a young man's house wearing something see-through. She had never been so blatant before and had to admit the thought turned her on. Maybe Chris Small would let her in straight away and they would have wild sex on that lumpy bed of his. The thought wasn't quite as off-putting as it had been on Monday.

She tried on several blouses, finally settling on a see-through black lace one with glittery patterns all over it so her nipples weren't quite so easy to see. He would be able to see them all right, but he would have to look quite hard. Then she put on a pair of black slacks, some black boots and a black jacket. She would leave the jacket open so, when he answered the door he could see her cleavage. Hopefully he would ask her in for a better look. That way, she felt less of a tart and it wouldn't be so blatant.

She picked up her handbag and walked out to the car. She

made the short drive to Elmhurst and once again, parked in the pub car park on the other side of the road from Small's place. Then she got out of the car, crossed the road, and walked to the high street.

She had worked out before that Chris Small's room was directly above the pet shop, on the second floor. There was another room between them, probably belonging to that gross-looking boy who had answered the door to her the other day, the one with the lump on his cheek. Looking up, she saw that both rooms had lights on so she wasn't going to be talked into going away tonight. She would force her way in if she had to. She walked back down the side street and walked up the stone steps to Chris Small's house.

Chris heard the bell ring and knew who it would be. After receiving the note from Rosetta, he knew it was only a matter of time before she turned up again. And this time he was quite keen to see her because he wanted to get a few things straightened out. He put on his slippers and went downstairs.

When he got to the bottom landing, Heavy Metal was standing there waiting for him. 'Looks like that blonde bit again,' he said. 'Want me to get rid of her?'

Chris shook his head. 'I'd better face her or this could go on forever.'

'Okay. Your call.'

Chris walked past him and opened the front door. Sure enough, it was Rosetta, dressed to kill.

'Hi there!' she said, with a big smile. 'We meet again. You're a hard man to get hold of.'

Chris stood back from the doorway. 'Come in. Let's go upstairs and talk.'

He watched her walk past him and then noticed that Heavy Metal was still standing there. Chris saw him giving Rosetta the once over, his eyes nearly popping out of his head. He shut the front door and followed behind, Heavy Metal giving him an envious look as he walked past.

Once inside his room, Rosetta took off her jacket and Chris now saw why Heavy Metal had been drooling. She was wearing a see-through blouse with nothing on underneath. Chris felt a stirring in his groin but forced himself to think of something else. He had got into trouble before by thinking with that particular part of his anatomy, and he didn't want to fall for it again. He told Rosetta to sit down on one of the metal chairs and then sat opposite her on the other one, the exact positions they had been in the other day. He decided to forget about the formalities and said, 'So what's going on, exactly?'

Rosetta tried acting innocent. 'What do you mean, what's going on?'

Chris stood up, turned to one of his bookshelves and opened a wooden box where he kept all his documents. He reached inside and brought out Dave Brill's business card. He handed it to Rosetta and watched her reaction. It was like she'd just been slapped in the face.

'I saw you with him the other day, Monday, about an hour after you'd been with me. You were sitting together in All Bar One in Bromley. It was a fluke I happened to be there at the same time, but I'd like to know how you know him. He tried getting into my flat some weeks ago. I don't know why. I do know that I don't trust him though, and now I don't trust you. So what's going on?'

He watched Rosetta put the card on the table. She suddenly looked her age. While she wasn't looking, he managed to sneak a look at her breasts. He couldn't see her nipples but he could see everything else. They looked in fine shape.

She looked up, almost catching him, and said, 'It's true, I do know him. Do you have anything to drink?'

'I don't normally keep drink in the room,' Chris said. 'We can go to the pub if you like, but dressed like that you may create a scene.'

Rosetta looked down at herself, as if noticing for the first time that she was near-enough naked. 'Have you got something I can put on underneath? Or on top?'

Chris went to his wardrobe and was embarrassed by the old clothes lying in there. 'How about a black T-shirt underneath?' He held one up in front of him.

'That'll be fine,' Rosetta said.

Then he watched in disbelief as she unbuttoned her blouse and took it off in front of him. He didn't know where to look but knew this might be his only chance. They were nice breasts too, and her nipples were erect.

He was glad he hadn't offered her a pullover.

24

IN THE PUB over the road, Rosetta told Chris the whole story. It all made perfect sense now. He sat through it feeling tense and was glad he had a drink to hand. So, Brill wanted revenge for what had happened in Boroughheath all those years ago. He might have known his shady past would come back to haunt him somewhere down the line. But who would have guessed it would happen nearly seven years later?

'So you came here tonight to lure me to your house for Sunday lunch, and Brill was going to beat me up there?' he asked.

'Not Dave. He's paying someone else to do it.'

'Great!' Chris said, a little too loudly. A few other drinkers turned to look at him. The pub was packed and he would put good money on it that he was the most pissed-off person there. And he had a right to be. He wanted to just walk away from Rosetta but felt he'd better stay and talk, try and find out more. 'And who is this other person? Not a hit man, I hope?'

'No. Even Dave wouldn't go that far. Just some guy he knows. A builder, I think. One that likes fighting.'

'Jesus Christ! That's all I need, a fight with a builder.'

'He wants him to break one of your limbs. An arm or a leg.'

'Charming! And you went along with all this? You strike me as having more intelligence than that.'

'I'm sorry,' Rosetta said. 'I don't know why I agreed to it. It seemed like a bit of fun at first. Now I'm not so sure. I am going to split up with Dave though. I feel so bad about it now. I should have dumped him a long time ago.'

Chris felt a little wary. Wasn't she changing her tune a little too quickly? He also felt a little sorry for her as well. A bored, middle-aged woman who had nothing better to do than concoct criminal plans with her boyfriend. 'I'll get us another drink,' he said.

Rosetta was drinking gin and tonic and Chris decided to have a whisky this time, along with another pint. He carried them back to the table and squeezed in beside her.

'All that stuff that happened to me in '91,' he said, 'none of that was really my fault. To begin with, I got mugged, and then I just wanted to find out who the perpetrator was. When I did, I sort of became friendly with him, and we tried getting some money out of his accomplice, from a mugging that he did. It all went badly wrong and they both ended up dead. But I wasn't responsible for it. It was just the way it turned out. My original mugger committed suicide, though, and I felt a bit bad about that. But the suicide was already in him. It was already in the family. I didn't put it there. I think it would've happened some-where down the line anyway. He was a very unhappy bloke.'

Rosetta nodded. 'I can understand suicide. Sometimes I get that way myself. I mean, what am I doing with my life? Wasting away in Sidcup, having an affair with a builder while my husband sends me monthly cheques. Most days, I have very little respect for myself. That's probably why I got mixed up in this. Maybe I wanted to get caught or something.'

'Maybe you wanted something to shock you into changing your life. Hoping that the worst would happen. Well it won't, because now I know about it.'

'So where do we go from here?'

'I don't know. I'll have to think about that one. Have you eaten yet tonight?'

Rosetta looked at him with surprise. 'No. Why?'

'There's a good Indian down the road and I haven't been to it for ages. I'll treat you.'

'Are you sure? After everything I've been trying to do to you?'

'I'm the forgiving type. And besides, it's Friday night.' Chris wondered if he was being truthful. Why exactly did he want to take Rosetta for a meal? Maybe it was the thought of her breasts. It would be nice to see those again before she left.

They chatted some more as they finished their drinks and then wandered down the road to the restaurant. Chris hadn't been there for years: not since his last stint in Elmhurst.

The restaurant was already three-quarters full and they were shown to a table at the back. They ordered more drinks and looked at the menu.

'This feels so strange,' Rosetta said. 'Dave never takes me out for meals in case he gets seen. In the two years I've been going out with him, we've had one weekend away and that's it. And here we are. Out for a meal straight away.'

'That's what happens when you go out with a married man. I'm always flabbergasted as to why women go out with them. You know it's a no-win situation and yet so many of you do it. What's the attraction?'

'Maybe it's because, deep down, we know they'll never leave their wives so therefore we're safe. There's no commitment.'

'But so many women get hurt by it. It bewilders me. I mean, you don't get that many single men going out with married women, do you?'

'No, you don't, but married women usually have kids and single men don't want to get involved in all that. And a woman's figure usually goes to pot when she's had kids. And men will always look at a woman's figure first.'

Chris felt himself blushing. He couldn't disagree with that.

A waiter came over, took their order, and then disappeared.

'Presumably you've never had kids?' Chris asked.

Rosetta laughed. 'I'm not as dumb as that. Why, do I look like I have?'

'No. You've got a great figure.'

'Thanks.'

'And you're what, in your late forties?'

Rosetta smiled. 'Haven't you learnt that's the question you never ask a woman?'

'I know that. But I always break the rules. I like to get things out in the open. I'm thirty-nine.'

Rosetta looked surprised. 'You look younger than that, but

it's so hard to tell these days. So you're four years older than Dave. I would have put it the other way round.'

'Well, he's married with kids and a mistress. That's bound to take its toll on your looks.'

'I never think of myself as a mistress, but I suppose I am.'

Eventually their meal arrived and they put the conversation aside for a while. They had chicken and lamb and a variety of vegetable dishes. Chris could never remember what he ate when he went to Indian restaurants, but whatever he had it always tasted good. He preferred it to Chinese food.

When the meal was finished, they ordered ice cream and sat back with full stomachs.

'Going back to the topic of kids,' Chris said. 'A few years ago when I was living in Brighton, I lodged with a woman who had a three-year-old. She was a lovely kid called Debbie, and the experience really opened my eyes.'

'Tell me more,' Rosetta said.

'Well, I'd always been skeptical about having kids, but Debbie was so cute and well-behaved, such a nice personality, I just fell for her. I played with her every evening, and loved every minute of it. Yet her mother, who was nine years younger than me, felt that by having a kid she was missing out on life. I felt the opposite. I think a kid fills up your life. When I finally left I was really upset because I knew I would never see Debbie again. And I haven't. I often wonder what she looks like now.'

'Why don't you go and visit?'

'I'm often tempted, but it's been so long, Debbie would probably have forgotten all about me.'

'Maybe not. You never know. And that's the secret of life, is it? Kids?'

'As far as I've been able to work out. I felt like I really belonged for once, and every evening I couldn't wait to get home. It was like a light had been turned on in my life. It certainly turned my head around.'

Rosetta laughed. 'Like in *The Exorcist*?'

Chris smiled. 'I can see my philosophy is wasted on you.'

He looked around the restaurant at other couples and groups. Everyone seemed to be having a fine time. 'Don't you ever get sick of living on your own?' he said.

Rosetta nodded. 'Many times. I've got a few friends I see now and again, but that's about it.'

'I've been living on my own since I was sixteen, when I left home, apart from two years with one woman. Sometimes I get home and think, well what do I do now? Is this how I'm going to spend the rest of my life?'

'At least you have a job,' Rosetta said. 'I have nothing; far too many hours during the day to get through. My life is framed around planning my next meal or TV. I sit with the *TV Times* and circle everything I'm going to watch that day.'

'I used to do that as well but I don't have a TV any more.'

'I noticed. What happened to it?'

'It was nicked. The whole house was robbed back in March. Now I just have a laptop computer.'

'What a pair we make.'

'Yeah. We're quite similar really.'

They finished their ice-creams, paid the bill and walked back up the road.

'I'm going to have to catch a taxi home,' Rosetta said. 'I'm way over the limit.' Chris noticed her swaying slightly as she walked.

'You'll have to ring from a call box then. No phones in my place as you know.'

'I have a mobile,' she said.

'I should have guessed.'

Rosetta laughed. 'But first I'll give you your T-shirt back.'

25

THEY LAY NAKED together in the single bed. The only sound was the occasional passing car and Chris still couldn't believe what had just happened. He had just had the best sex of his life – but now he was dying for a pee.

Rosetta was flaked out beside him and he'd have to climb over. He didn't want to wake her though, so first he replayed what had just happened, wondering if it was all just a drunken dream.

They had come back to his flat, both more than a little drunk, and Rosetta had once again peeled off her blouse before taking off Chris's black T-shirt. This time he had been drawn to her breasts like a magnet and within seconds, his mouth had been clamped to them, Rosetta urging him on.

Then his lips had found hers, and although it had been strange kissing an older woman, he had soon got used to it and they'd started undressing each other slowly. They had slid under the covers of the cold little bed and Rosetta had led him all the way. She knew how to do things slowly and her hands seemed to touch every part of him before they landed on the parts he really wanted her to touch. By that time, he was going crazy with desire and almost came in her hands. But she was patient with him and let him calm down, before leading him into her body.

They made love in a stop, start fashion – it was the only way Chris could hold back – and when he couldn't hold back any longer he thought his insides were going to burst.

They fell asleep, locked together, before he rolled off to his present position. And he still couldn't get her hands out of his mind; those long slender fingers teasing every inch of him. Jesus! He'd never experienced anything like that before. But he had to go and pee.

He squeezed himself out from beside her and climbed over her body. He took his dressing gown from the hook on the door and walked, barefoot, downstairs to the bathroom. He relieved himself, then had a quick wash in the sink. When he looked in the mirror, he was amazed to see he still looked the same.

The rest of the night was a restless one; Rosetta's body bumping into his, Chris never getting comfortable enough to sleep for long periods. And when he did wake up he just thought of those hands again and started getting hard. He couldn't wait for morning to see if they could have another go. But maybe when she was sober, she wouldn't want him so much. So he lay awake and worried about that as well.

Eventually, he sensed the morning light creeping into the room, and then Rosetta's body climbing out of bed. He saw her leave the room in his dressing gown and then, five minutes later, she was back in bed next to him. Then he felt those fingers again, running up and down his body, so he turned her face towards him and kissed her.

In the light of the morning he was able to see her body much better and it was almost as good as some of the younger women he'd had. When he turned her over, her buttocks were in fine shape and her legs were hard and bony. Athletic looking, although she hadn't told him about taking any kind of exercise. He couldn't believe a woman of her age could look so good.

Once again, he felt like his insides were going to explode and they lay together afterwards in each other's arms. He waited for his breathing to get back to normal and then said, 'That was the best breakfast I've ever had.'

'So what do we do now?' Rosetta asked. She had a splitting headache and was starting to think of Dave Brill and what she would say to him.

'Do you want to try again?' Chris said, and she sensed he was only half joking.

'I was looking at the bigger picture and what to do about Dave.'

'Let me think about it for a moment.'

She lay there quietly and thought about their lovemaking. It made a nice change to have a man on top of her who wasn't overweight, like Dave. And energetic, too. Chris's mouth had been all over her like a leech. Was there any part of her he hadn't kissed or licked? She couldn't think of any.

Eventually, Chris said to her, 'Here's what we do.' She listened while he told her his simple plan and she didn't see why it wouldn't work.

She felt relieved after that and went under the sheets to seek him out with her mouth. A man like this deserved to be taken care of properly.

About an hour later, Chris was dressed and ready for work. He stood and watched Rosetta as she applied a little make-up around her eyes, then gave her a final hug and kiss before walking downstairs with her.

When they reached the bottom landing, Heavy Metal was walking along with a plate full of beans, bacon and toast. His heavy metal girlfriend was tagging along behind, carrying a plate of the same. They were both wearing heavy metal T-shirts and pyjama bottoms.

'Way to go,' Heavy Metal mumbled as he walked past, and Chris couldn't help but smile.

When they reached the front door, Chris looked out of the window next to the kitchen, into the pub car park. He didn't trust Brill one little bit and half expected his BMW to be parked there.

'Looks like the coast is clear,' he said.

They stepped outside and walked over the road to Rosetta's Audi. There was a piece of paper stuck under her windscreen wipers and Chris took it and read out loud:

'This car park is for the use of patrons only. Please don't park here again.'

'That's a relief,' Rosetta said. 'I thought it was a message from Dave.'

They climbed inside and Rosetta drove Chris to Elmhurst station. He kissed her goodbye and ran through the underground tunnel, just in time to catch his train. When he was sitting on board, he slumped into his seat and closed his eyes. Now he truly knew the meaning of the term 'shagged out.'

When Rosetta got home she sat in the living room and rang Dave Brill on his mobile. He didn't sound his usual cocky self. He sounded a bit depressed.

'So how did it go?' he asked.

'Success at last,' she said. 'He invited me in for a while and has agreed to come round for Sunday lunch.'

'That's great,' Dave said, though not with the enthusiasm she'd expected. 'What time?'

'He's coming at twelve, so get here around two. That'll give me enough time to fill him with food and wine. He'll be like a dopy puppy dog for you.'

'That's my girl. So the sexy clothes did the trick then?'

'Seems so. I wore that black lacy thing with the silver patterns on it.'

'A good choice. Maybe you could wear it for me sometime.'

'If you're a good boy,' Rosetta said, sensing there was still something different about Dave's voice. Maybe he was just a little hungover.

They talked a while longer and then she hung up. She went upstairs and ran a hot bath. She didn't feel guilty, telling lies to Dave at all. She had almost forgotten him already and was looking forward to her next meeting with Chris. She felt, at last, that her life was going in a new and exciting direction.

26

AFTER STRUGGLING THROUGH work on Saturday, but then getting an early night, Chris felt back to normal by Sunday, when he went to work to sack Hugh. He got there early and waited by the front door, sitting on a stack of Heineken.

Ten minutes before opening time, he saw Hugh approaching from the other side of the road. He didn't look both ways before crossing, an obvious sign of cockiness as far as Chris was concerned. Then he saw the look of surprise when Hugh realised that one of the lights was on.

Chris unlocked the front door and let him in. Hugh looked at him warily and could only say, 'What are you doing here?'

Chris said, 'I think we need to chat.'

They stood and looked at each other and neither of them moved.

'Okay,' Hugh said. 'Fire away.'

Chris almost laughed out loud. 'You don't know how right you are.'

'Pardon?' Hugh said, looking puzzled.

So Chris told him about the security guard from Marks & Spencer, Hugh's face turning through various stages of embarrassment, innocence, bitterness, and then finally aggression.

'So you're going to believe a total stranger instead of me?' he said, at the end of it.

'He's not exactly a total stranger. He's a regular customer.'

'Well fuck him.'

'And I also checked with Hamleys. They said you were sacked for the same thing.'

Hugh didn't have an answer to that one.

'So, if you'll give me the keys you can be on your way.'

Chris watched as Hugh tried thinking of something clever

to say – some kind of parting shot – but all he could come up with was, 'You haven't heard the last of this.'

Chris smiled. 'Yeah, I've heard that one before.'

Then, Hugh handed over the keys and marched towards the front door. Then he realised he would have to wait for Chris to let him out, so he just stood there, looking stupid.

'So don't I get paid for today?' he asked, as Chris unlocked the door.

Chris laughed. 'You've got to be joking.'

He opened the door and, as Hugh walked out, he swore at Chris under his breath. Chris almost pulled him back in to beat the shit out of him, but he couldn't be bothered. He had more important things to worry about. He closed the door and got ready for his Sunday shift.

Rosetta spent the morning cooking a Sunday lunch for two. She knew all along that she would be the only one eating it but she had to make it look good. She dressed in a strapless, slinky red dress and a pair of high heels, tarting herself up for the date that would never arrive.

Then she sat in the living room with a glass of white wine, watching TV, flicking through the channels trying to find something decent to watch. She felt a little nervous inside, wondering what Dave would say when she told him that Chris hadn't turned up.

Dave Brill sat in his BMW, outside Sidcup station, looking at his watch. The train Luke had said he'd be on had already come and gone. He sat there swearing to himself and decided to wait for the next one. He was feeling more than a little tense about the whole situation.

Yesterday morning, still feeling hungover from the meal with friends on Friday night, he had jumped in his BMW and driven round to Rosetta's house to ask what had happened with Chris Small. Her Audi wasn't parked in its usual spot, so on a hunch he drove to Chris Small's place and, lo and behold, there was her car, sitting in the pub car park. Brill had almost run down a wandering cat, he was so shocked and disappointed, but then parked his car instead and stuck a note on Rosetta's windscreen.

Then, later in the day, she had had the gall to ring and tell him it was all set up for today. He could tell by her voice she was lying to him. He was pretty certain something had happened on Friday night in Small's flat. Maybe she had fucked him. That was a thought that made his blood boil even more, and now he had a double reason for breaking one of the limbs of Chris Small. That's if Luke, the limb-breaker ever turned up.

Twenty minutes later he saw Luke ambling towards him, the six-foot-two beanpole with the scruffy beard. He was wearing faded jeans, windbreaker and trainers, and carrying something in a long canvas tent-bag. Brill leaned over, opened the passenger door and watched as Luke climbed in.

'What's in the bag?' he asked.

'The weapon of destruction,' Luke said.

'Which is?'

'A baseball bat.'

Brill started the car and said, 'I thought you were going to be on the last train.'

'You're lucky I'm here at all.'

'Why? Because of your beloved football match?'

'Too right. I hope we get finished before it starts.'

'We probably can. Does it start at four?'

'Yeah.'

'So we'll be well finished by then. I'll drop you at a pub and you can watch it there. Okay?'

'Yeah, fine.'

But Brill could tell Luke's mind wasn't a hundred per cent focused on the job ahead.

Rosetta waited until one o'clock and then rang Dave on his mobile.

'What's up?' he said.

'He's not here.'

'And why do you think that is?'

'I can't read his mind, can I?'

'I'm coming in,' Dave said.

Rosetta put the phone down and waited nervously. Then she heard a car pulling up outside and a door opening and closing. Then Dave was putting his key in the front door and coming in.

She looked up from the sofa and felt a little scared of his size this time: that big stomach, the round face and the stubble on his chin. How on earth had she ever fancied him? She watched him walk over and sit down opposite. He was wearing smart jeans and a nice clean shirt, all spruced up for the little bit of violence he hoped would happen today.

'So what's going on?' he asked.

Rosetta took a deep breath. 'He hasn't turned up. He obviously isn't coming.' She waved her hand at the table set for two. Brill just looked at her and shook his head.

'You'll have to do better than that,' he said. 'You've never been a good liar, Rosetta.'

Rosetta knew she wasn't a good liar as well. She looked down at her red dress and knew there wasn't any point in carrying on with the charade. The original plan had been to tell Dave that Chris obviously wasn't interested in her as he hadn't turned up, and then say that she'd done her best, it wasn't going to work, and she wanted to drop out of his little game. Now she might have to tell him everything.

'I'm opting out of this, Dave,' she said. 'I spent the evening with Chris Small and I think you're way off the mark. He's a nice man and I don't want anything to do with causing him harm. And if something does happen to him I'll know who to send the police to.'

Dave looked at her with a sneer but was calmer than she expected him to be. 'Oh yeah?' was all he could say.

'Yeah. And I want my house keys back, and I don't want to see you again.'

Dave nodded slowly, his face becoming a stony mask, not letting anything show. She watched as he pulled out his keys and dropped them on the coffee table. Then he stood up and walked towards the door. Rosetta couldn't believe this was so easy.

At the door, he turned and said, 'Did you fuck him? I saw your car parked outside his place this morning. I put that note on your windscreen.'

Now Rosetta knew why he was acting so calm. He had already come to the conclusion that it was over. She didn't want to tell him she'd slept with Chris – that was the last thing she wanted him to know. But before she could help herself, she felt it slipping out. 'Yes I did actually,' she said quietly. 'And I enjoyed it. It seems like your plan has backfired quite badly.'

She watched Dave nod, waited for him to say something, but he didn't. Once again his quiet reaction was the complete opposite of what she'd expected. He nodded again and then walked out.

Luke sat in the BMW and wondered what was going on. He looked at his watch. Twenty-past one. He wanted to get stuck in, though there was still plenty of time before the match started.

Then he saw Dave marching down the street towards him. He looked in a foul mood. He opened the driver's door, climbed in, and sat in stony silence.

'Something wrong?' Luke asked.

'Too fucking right it's wrong,' Dave said.

Luke looked at him. He was all worked up like a bull. He could almost see steam coming from his nose. Maybe he should wear a ring in it. He had to stifle a laugh.

'What's so fucking funny?' Dave snarled.

'Nothing. Just thinking of other things.'

'Like football? You'll have plenty of time for your match now.'

'Why? Isn't it going to happen today?'

'No, it's a complete balls-up.'

'Well, what are you waiting for? Get me to the station.'

He watched as Dave started the car. They drove along in silence for a while and then Dave said, 'You know, I've figured it out about you football freaks.'

Luke didn't even bother to answer; he knew he was going to get slagged off whatever he said. That happened at work sometimes. If something went wrong it was always his fault, never Dave's.

'You all go to the pub,' Dave said, 'and watch these matches because you're scared of missing something. Most of the games, and you have to admit it, are a load of shite. So you all go along, hoping that the next match is *the* match, *the* one you'll all be talking about for years to come. And you know what the sad thing is?'

Luke didn't even bother looking at him.

'The sad thing is, you'll only get one of these great matches every season, so you'll have to sit through forty or fifty just to see it. Now I find that fucking sad.'

Luke still didn't bother answering him. He wasn't even listening. He was just glad he'd be able to get back to Camden, back to JD's Sportsbar, and watch from his regular seat.

The car pulled up in front of the station and Dave said, 'It's just you and me now, Luke. Rosetta's out of the picture.'

Luke couldn't be bothered talking about it now. 'Any chance of expenses?' he asked. 'It's not cheap coming all the way down here.'

Then he watched with satisfaction as Dave reached in a pocket and pulled out a ten-pound note.

Luke took it, opened the door, and said, 'See you.'

27

AS HE LOCKED up the shop and headed for the West End on Sunday evening, Chris felt in a pretty good mood, despite the earlier sacking of Hugh and having to work his first Sunday for about eight weeks. It had been a busy day, and he always felt satisfied when he took a lot of money through the till.

On Saturday he had received a phone call from Edie, asking if he fancied going to the casinos tonight. Still suffering from his hangover, he had been reluctant to agree, but now that the Sunday shift was over he was quite pleased to be going out on the town. After all, tomorrow was his day off and he could have a long lie-in if he wanted to.

He had rung Rosetta earlier in the evening and asked what had happened with Brill. She told him that he'd taken her bad news very calmly, even the part about them sleeping together, because he'd suspected it already. She told him about the note on her car. She thought that would be the end of the matter. Chris doubted it somehow.

The way he figured it, Brill would be even more upset now he knew Rosetta had been unfaithful. She should have told him that she just wanted to drop out of his little game and left it at that, but no; she had to go and tell him the whole story. But then again, if Brill had seen her car at his place maybe telling him was the only thing to do.

Then Rosetta had asked Chris when she could see him again and, despite some reservations, he quite fancied the idea. Her long fingers, and the way they had taunted and teased him, was still fresh in his mind, and he couldn't wait to have a second go when they were both sober and more awake. He said he would ring her tomorrow.

When he got to The Angel pub he found Brad sitting there

on his own. He sat down and asked where Edie was.

'She's come down with a cold,' he said. 'Just hit her overnight. I didn't fancy staying indoors so I thought the two of us could have a go tonight.'

'Okay,' Chris said. 'But who's going to do the card counting?'

'Me. I've been brushing up over the past few weeks.'

Chris nodded. 'That must be why you're drinking Coke.'

'That's right,' Brad said. 'I also brought you a balance sheet.' He reached in an inside pocket and gave him a folded piece of paper. 'Our results so far.'

Chris looked at the sheet, neatly typed and printed on graph paper. It had the names and dates of the casinos they'd visited, then a total of how much they'd won or lost each evening. The balance at the bottom said they were £450 up.

'That's a pretty big total,' Chris said. 'More than I thought.'

'But not so big divided three ways.'

'That's a point. But it's a start.'

They left a few minutes later, walked to the Underground at Tottenham Court Road, and caught a tube to Green Park. They walked through the smart Mayfair area to Hertford Street and entered the Colonial Casino ten minutes apart. It was one of Chris's least favourite casinos, but as Brad was doing the counting, he had the choice.

Once again, Chris found himself at the bar, sitting with a Coke, waiting for the signal to play. He saw Brad on the other side of the room facing him, at a table that didn't have many spare seats. It took fifteen minutes or so for Brad to link his hands behind his neck, and Chris wandered over.

He sat down and played his Basic Strategy, hardly thinking about it at all these days, and feeling even more relaxed because Edie wasn't around. He always felt a little tense playing with her because she would be in such a bad mood if they lost, and that always added more pressure. Brad, on the other hand, was more easy-going and they got on well, so it was an entirely different experience. He watched Brad's left hand rest-ing on the table, and waited for the usual signals.

The signals eventually came and Chris started altering his bets. He won some big money on a couple of split hands and then on some double downs. Everything was going so smoothly that a pit boss came over and stood in front of the table, watching. He was a tough-looking guy with a broken nose and slicked-back hair. Chris decided to back down. He placed a few small stupid bets until the boss disappeared and then got the signal from Brad to leave. He got up and left the table.

He cashed in his chips and counted a hundred and sixty pounds profit in just under an hour. He left the casino and waited outside in a bus shelter for Brad.

'Easy money,' Brad said when he came out. He slapped Chris on the back and they both laughed. They decided to have a drink to celebrate.

Seated in a pub, Chris handed over his winnings under the table. 'I felt more relaxed with you,' he said. 'Edie's so intense she puts me on edge.'

'I know what you mean. She just wants to win so bad. She'll be pleased we won tonight, though.'

'Will we have to split this three ways or two?' Chris asked, half joking.

'Three, I guess. I don't think Edie would take it too kindly any other way.'

'She deserves it, anyway. She's been putting in all the hard work so far.'

Brad nodded. 'In real pro American teams, the counter will always get a bigger percentage than the hammer men. In a team of three, she'd probably get fifty per cent while we'd get twenty-five each.'

'Shit. She can definitely have some then.' Chris took a swig of his pint. He felt like going to another casino right away, but guessed it was better to quit while they were ahead. 'Do you want to try a twosome some other time?' he asked.

'Tomorrow's your day off, isn't it?'

'Yeah. But Tuesday would be all right. That's if Edie's still

ill. She won't be too pleased if we strike out on our own.'

Brad laughed. 'She'd be fuming. Let's see if she's still ill on Tuesday. I'll give you a ring.'

Chris took another sip of beer and said, 'You'll never believe what happened to me the other night,' and then told Brad about his wild night of sex with Rosetta. He left out the part about Dave Brill and just said he'd met Rosetta when she'd offered to drive him and his gas bottle to another shop, which was more or less the truth anyway. When he'd finished, he asked, 'Have you ever slept with an older woman before?'

Brad nodded. 'The old cliché I'm afraid. I slept with my best friend's mother when I was eighteen.'

'Tell me more,' Chris said.

'She was a great-looking woman. Her name was Liana. Very attractive with long ginger hair, a nice figure, and a great personality. I was working locally at the time and she lived just three doors down. I used to drop in and see her after work and we'd have very long chats. Her husband worked very odd hours, some sort of computer salesman. The chats got longer and longer and one evening we just ended up in bed.'

'And where was your best friend?'

'He was away at college. The affair only lasted a few months, it was just too risky. But it was great while it lasted.'

'And was she good in bed?'

'Well, I enjoyed it, although I didn't have anything to compare it with at the time. In hindsight, I think it all comes down to experience, not age, and she had only slept with her husband. That's not going to make you into the world's greatest lover.'

'I suppose not.'

'I once went out with this girl, she was a couple of years younger than me, and she always gave the impression of being Little Miss Innocent. When I finally got her into bed it was a totally different story. Man, was she hot! Knew a lot of moves I'd never tried before. Unfortunately, I only had sex with her about four times but they were the best I've ever had. I later found out that she slept around a lot at school and so she'd learnt from experience. It sure made a big difference.'

Chris smiled. 'Maybe that's why Rosetta was so good. She really knew what to do with her hands. So, maybe the answer is that we should all sleep around a bit more; brush up on our technique.'

'A bit risky these days,' Brad said. 'It all comes down to education though. Most people stumble through their sex lives, never learning anything about it. I think that's particularly true about the English. What you need to do is read some books, watch some videos, and it makes the world of difference. Most people don't bother.'

Chris had to agree. Even at the age of thirty-nine he was never confident he was doing the right thing with a woman. Maybe he would buy a video. Then he remembered that he didn't have a video any more. Maybe a few more sessions with Rosetta would improve his technique. He could ask her where she learnt it.

He went to the bar and bought another round. It felt good being out with Brad, without Edie, and it again reminded him of what a solitary life he led. He would have to look to ways of improving it, of being a more sociable person, but he'd never been that sociable anyway, all through his life.

They left after the second pint and walked back to Charing Cross. There was a fast train to Orpington just about to leave so Brad said goodbye and ran for it.

Chris waited on the concourse with a ragbag collection of people, most of them half drunk, going home to sleep off the weekend before another humdrum week of work faced them. Chris was glad he had the next day off.

A few homeless people stumbled around, asking for money, and two of them came towards him. He was used to this. Standing alone on a station, not looking too threatening, homeless people always made a beeline for him. He gave them both fifty pence just to get rid of them, then caught the next train home.

28

AS IT WAS now the beginning of May and spring was in the air, Chris decided the next day that it was time to take the Plasticine from the gaps in his windows so that, once again, he could open them and get some fresh air into his room. After finishing breakfast, he pulled the metal table away from the wall and started peeling away.

He noticed that the wall below the window was stained black with more damp than usual, so later he would have to clean it with hot water and bleach, his usual method of getting rid of fungus. He looked down at the passing traffic as he dug the Plasticine out with a butter knife.

When all the Plasticine was removed he turned the latch on the left-hand window and tried easing it open. Nothing happened. He tried the window on the right but that was stuck as well.

He went to the wardrobe and fetched a large screwdriver from his toolbox. He inserted it into a gap near the latch and, after a few minutes of leverage, gently managed to ease the window open. He stood there with a nice, cool breeze coming through but was now worried that maybe he wouldn't be able to get the window shut. So he pulled the window towards him, and just as he feared, it wouldn't fit.

He swore out loud and started sweating. He couldn't spend the whole spring with a window that wouldn't shut; he would have to try harder.

He spent the next five minutes struggling away, but just couldn't get the damned thing back in. Maybe it would be easier with two people. He went down the hallway and knocked on John's door.

John answered, still in his dressing gown and pyjamas.

Chris told him the trouble he was having and John agreed to help. He followed him along the corridor in his slippers.

'Blimey,' John said, looking around Chris's room. 'There's nothing in here.'

Chris was a little taken aback. 'Well, most of it was nicked,' he said.

'Fair enough,' John said.

Chris showed him the window. 'I thought if one of us pulled on the latch and the other worked with the screwdriver we could squeeze it back in. You're probably stronger than I am so how about if you pull the latch?'

John jokingly flexed his right bicep. 'Right. Ready.' He stood to Chris's left, holding the latch, and started pulling.

Chris inserted the screwdriver, trying to ease the old wood frame back in. They struggled for a few minutes and John said, 'I feel it moving. I think it's going back in.'

Chris sensed something moving as well and inserted the screwdriver harder. It was making a few dents in the window frame but that didn't worry him. After a few more minutes the window started squeezing in. 'Keep going,' he said. 'One hard pull should do it.'

He dropped his screwdriver on the floor, put his hands around John's, and tugged on the latch as well. The window started to move but then there was a horrible scraping sound.

The next thing Chris knew, they were both falling backwards, with the whole window frame falling on top of them. They landed on their backs with a crash and some of the window shattered. John gave a cry for help, and when Chris looked up, all he could see was a great big hole in the wall and the tree outside.

Then there was a gust of wind, and one of the branches broke free and poked itself into the room.

'Fucking hell,' Chris said. 'That's all I need.'

He lifted the window frame up, squeezed out from underneath, then held it up for John to get out. They brushed themselves down and looked for any cuts.

'Well, I'm okay,' John said. 'I thought I was a goner there.'

'Me too,' Chris said. 'But no cuts on me either.'

They stepped over the broken glass to the gaping hole. The bricks around the window were loose and flaky, and Chris picked one off and dropped it on the floor. The cement between the bricks was non-existent, more like sand. He poked his head out, looked down at the street below, and saw several people looking up at them.

'Can you call the police for me?' Chris shouted down to them. One of them nodded and walked quickly down the street.

Chris pulled his head back in and looked at John. 'I always knew it was too damp in here,' he said. 'Now I know why. The whole building is rotting.'

John looked at him with concern. 'I wonder if my room is the same?'

About ten minutes later, a policeman turned up, the same one Chris had spoken to the day his room had been robbed. Larry somebody. He looked at Chris with a wry smile and said, 'You don't seem to be having much luck here.'

Then he walked over to the hole in the wall and looked out at the view. Chris explained what had happened, while Larry shook his head in disbelief.

'You'll have to leave the premises, I would think,' he said, when Chris had finished. 'Have you anywhere you can go?'

Chris shook his head. 'Not that I can think of.'

'I'll get the fire brigade over and you'd better notify your landlord.'

'Landlady, as I told you before. The lord lives somewhere in Spain.'

'I'm not surprised.'

'Someone's already gone to ring her,' Chris said. 'What about the other residents? Will they have to move out too?'

'Let's see what the fire brigade say.'

There was a fire station less than a mile away so it didn't

take long for a truck to pull up outside. A large crowd had gathered in the street and Chris was worried that the local paper would turn up as well, no doubt with a photographer. He had a phobia about local newspapers ever since his last appearance in them. He was also worried about where he was going to sleep that night.

Two firemen in uniform appeared in the room and looked at the mess. They had a good laugh and joke about it, and Chris smiled as well to keep them happy.

'Wall-tie degradation,' one of them said. 'That's usually what the problem is in these old houses.'

The other one nodded and turned to Chris. 'The whole house will have to be evacuated.'

Larry turned to Chris and said, 'I should ask for your deposit back if I were you.'

Chris packed up his clothes in two suitcases, and all his other belongings in a cardboard box. Then he walked down the hall to John's room. He was dressed now and packing up as well.

'I don't see why I can't stay,' John moaned. 'It doesn't mean the whole house is going to fall down.'

Chris could see he was upset. 'Sorry, John. Do you have anywhere you can go?'

'My brother's coming to pick me up. I'll stay with him a while.'

Chris asked if he needed any help but sensed he was in the way. He went downstairs and found Heavy Metal and his girlfriend chatting in the hall with Larry.

'I don't see why we can't stay,' Heavy Metal was saying. 'We're a floor below, for God's sake.'

Chris squeezed past them, walked out of the front door and down the steps, and into the pub opposite. He made two phone calls; one of them to a taxi firm. He'd already figured where he was going to stay but he had to check if they had any rooms. He wondered what it would be like going back there. He hadn't set foot in the place for seven years.

29

DAVE BRILL SPENT most of Monday in a bad mood. He was still smarting after being given the elbow by Rosetta, but had the sense to apologise to Luke for his rudeness the day before. He told Luke about how Chris Small had now taken his woman as well. Luke didn't seem to care one way or the other. Brill asked him how the Arsenal match had gone and Luke had told him it was a 0-0 draw. Brill nodded. It merely confirmed his theory about football but he kept his mouth shut.

They spent all day on the roof together, working on yet another chimney. Then they ate their lunches separately: Luke on the ground, Brill on the roof looking out over the back gardens. He would have to find himself another woman now that Rosetta was out of the picture, and he scanned the houses, hoping to see a nice-looking one. He still couldn't contemplate life without her, and more importantly, life without her body. Where on earth was he going to find a woman who satisfied him so much? It felt like the end of an era.

When they were back working together in the afternoon Brill brought up the subject of Chris Small once again. 'I'm going to raise your hit money,' he said, out of the blue.

Luke looked at him with surprise. 'I thought all that was over with. I thought you'd lost interest.'

Brill shook his head. 'My interest merely dipped for a few hours. In fact, now it's more intense. I can't bear the thought he's taken my woman as well. He deserves to be done in even more. I'm raising your money to a thousand.'

Luke almost whistled at the amount. 'A thousand! Now you're talking. I'd even half kill him for that.'

'No need. Just something broken. Although I wouldn't mind if you broke his head instead of his arm.'

Luke nodded excitedly. 'I can do heads.'

Brill smiled for the first time that day. 'Good man. After work, I'll show you where he lives and you can take it from there.'

Luke nodded his head. 'A thousand pounds!'

Chris stood in his new room, his two suitcases on the bed, his cardboard box on the floor. He didn't know whether to laugh or cry.

He was on the first floor this time, looking out over the front drive; the football pitch surrounded by the high wire fence, and then the main road. Nothing had changed.

It brought back a lot of old feelings and he wondered how good it was, psychologically, for him to be back here, but where else could he have gone? He had nowhere. The only other place he could think of was Rosetta's and he didn't want to get into that situation so soon. No, this would just have to do for the moment. He would find somewhere else as soon as possible.

As he unpacked, he found it all very strange. When the taxi had brought him down the YMCA drive he had felt his spirits sinking. The last time he'd been in a car on that same stretch of road he'd been going the other way, being taken away by the police. He hadn't known then what his fate would be and he didn't know now what his fate would be. Just being back gave him a feeling of trepidation, and most of those feelings were attached to the thought of Dave Brill. But then again, now that he was living somewhere different how was Brill going to find him? He relaxed a little as he hung up his shirts in the wardrobe.

An hour later he went downstairs to the lobby and rang Rosetta on one of the payphones. He told her what had happened and asked if she'd like to come over and see his new abode. 'I need some cheering up,' he added.

'A YMCA,' Rosetta said. 'That'll be a new experience.'

He told her the number of his room and went back upstairs to wait.

He sat at the desk in front of the window so he'd be able to see when she arrived. He looked at the cars streaming by on the main road, just over a hundred yards away. The bus stop was still there, the one where he'd first met and chatted up Liz all those years ago. He wondered what she was up to now. He could get up early tomorrow and see if she was still turning up at the bus stop. It would be quite amusing to walk up the road towards her, see what her reaction would be, say hello like they were frozen in time.

Half an hour later, he saw Rosetta's Audi coming down the drive, then disappearing towards the parking area around the back. He went downstairs to the lobby and saw her walking up the back path. She was dressed in leggings again, just like the first time they'd met, and also her short brown suede jacket. He wondered what she was wearing underneath.

He gave her a kiss on the cheek as she entered and she gave him a big smile. 'You bring me to all the finest places,' she said.

They walked through the lobby, getting a few looks from some of the residents. They probably thought Rosetta was his mother. When he'd checked in a few hours ago he hadn't recognised any of the personnel, and luckily no one had recognised him. He was sure he was going to bump into someone though, maybe in the canteen at meal time.

He led Rosetta upstairs to his room. She gave it the once-over and said, 'Well at least it hasn't got any damp.'

Like Chris's last YMCA room, this one too had a wardrobe on the left as you walked in, and then a single bed. On the right was a basin and in front of the window was a long desk, with one grey plastic chair in front of it. There was also a green armchair.

'What's the bed like?' Rosetta asked.

'I haven't tried it yet,' Chris said.

Rosetta slowly undid her suede jacket and pulled it open. She wasn't wearing anything underneath.

'Well what are we waiting for?' she said.

*

After work, Dave Brill told Luke he would drive him to Elmhurst station so he could catch the train home to London. He also wanted to show him where Chris Small lived. They were driving up Elmhurst High Street, just approaching Small's house, when Brill glanced out of his window and said, 'What the fuck!'

He pulled the Toyota Hiace quickly to the curb and looked out of the window to the other side of the road.

'What is it?' Luke asked.

'A fucking great big hole in the wall!' Brill said.

Luke leaned over so he could see. 'So what?'

'That's where Small lives.'

Luke looked again. 'Looks like lover man might have moved out, then.'

Brill didn't like Small being referred to as lover man but didn't say anything. 'Unfortunately, you're probably right. You stay here. I'll see what I can find out.'

Brill put on the parking lights and climbed out. He crossed the road and walked into the pet shop. He nearly gagged at the smell of so many animals, but walked up to the back counter where a man in brown overalls stood. 'What happened to the wall?' he asked, pointing upwards.

The man took a deep breath. 'For the hundredth time. From what I understand, the young man living there opened the window and it fell out.'

Being a builder, Brill found that quite unusual. 'Yeah? Not on to the street, I hope.'

The man shook his head. 'No, back into the room. Everyone's been evacuated.'

'You mean the whole house is empty?'

'That's right.'

'Shit. You don't know where they've gone, do you? I've got a friend living there.'

'Haven't got a clue, I'm afraid. Maybe there's a note on the door.'

'Yeah,' Brill said. Then he found himself glancing in some

of the cages. He saw hamsters and gerbils, and a few noisy birds squawking away.

'Are you interested in buying a pet?' the man asked.

Brill shook his head. 'No, no thanks. I've already got two kids.' Then he turned and left.

He walked around to the back of the building and up the steps to the green door. There were no messages stuck there, so he rang all the bells. No reply. He swore and walked back down to the street.

As he jumped in the Toyota, Luke said to him, 'Well?'

'Our prey has disappeared.'

'Shit,' Luke said. 'I was looking forward to that thousand pounds.'

Brill looked at him. 'I wouldn't give up just yet,' he said. 'I'll think of something.'

30

THE NEXT MORNING, Tuesday, Chris got up early, slipped on his clothes, and went down to the canteen. He walked in and it was like nothing had changed. There were about twenty youngsters, ministry of defence workers, eating their breakfasts and chatting; and then a smattering of older men, life's temporary flotsam, sitting separately with their heads bowed over their plates.

He grabbed a tray and walked over to the serving area. He collected a cooked breakfast of beans, bacon, eggs and fried bread, a glass of orange juice and a cup of tea. He didn't recognise any of the staff. 'What happened to Marvin?' he asked, half-heartedly.

'Who's Marvin?' the server asked.

'A small guy with a harelip. He was working here last time I was here. About seven years ago.'

'Beats me,' the man said. 'I've only been here a couple of years.'

'Fair enough,' Chris said. He picked up his tray, ready to move off.

'Marvin's dead.' The voice came from another man. He was stacking clean cutlery in a rack, to Chris's right. Chris turned towards him. 'He cut his wrists with a carving knife. Happened about five years ago.'

'Shit. Sorry to hear that.'

'I guess he just didn't like being small.'

Chris nearly made a pun about his own surname, but thanked the man instead and walked away. He found a table by himself and sat down to eat.

After breakfast, he changed into his dressing gown and went down the hallway to the shower room. He still remembered how good the showers here were, and he locked himself in a cubicle and let the strong water wash over him. He thought back to his last YMCA shower. Liz had been outside waiting for him and they'd made love back in his room. Then he'd walked up the road with her and bumped into Rachel coming the other way. He hadn't been flavour of the month at that precise moment. He wondered what would happen after this shower.

He went back to his room and got dressed for the day. He felt a little horny, thinking back to yesterday's session with Rosetta. Once again her technique had amazed him. She was an inventive sexual artiste. Afterwards, he had treated her to a meal in a local pub. She had kept to the soft drinks before driving home around eight. Then Chris had gone to bed at ten, after an hour on the laptop with his blackjack game.

Chris hurriedly tied his shoes, remembering that he was now even farther away from Elmhurst station and would have to leave earlier for work. The eighteen-minute walk would now be nearer twenty-five or thirty. He locked his room and went downstairs. Already the maids were beginning their rounds.

About twenty minutes after he arrived at work, Chris realised that Sunday's takings had disappeared. Because the shop didn't have a safe, the money was kept in a brown paper bag at the bottom of a filing cabinet. He walked into the back room to get some extra five-pound notes for the till and the bag wasn't there. He looked around the storeroom, wondering if he'd put it somewhere else. After ten minutes of sweating and searching, he realised where it had gone. He went back in the shop and rang the police.

Forty-five minutes later, two policemen ambled in and he told them what had happened. 'I sacked a guy on Sunday for nicking money from the till and I bet it's him. He must have made a spare set of keys and come back in yesterday for it.'

One of the policemen held up his right hand. 'Steady on,

now, before we start making accusations. Now why do you think it was him?'

Chris went through the whole story again more slowly, while one of them made notes. Then Chris noticed a gap on the shelf right next to him. 'And add to that five bottles of Stolichnaya as well. The fucker's nicked my best vodka. Pardon my French.'

The policemen looked at each other. Chris reckoned they were both younger than him.

'And how much money in total was taken?'

Chris held up Sunday's till roll. 'Well, the whole day's takings came to eight hundred and fifty-two quid. Quite good for a Sunday. In a normal shop the credit cards would have been saved because they'd already have been entered into a PDQ machine. Unfortunately, we still do them the old way.' Chris held up his manual credit card machine. 'So I've lost the whole lot. They were in a bag with the money and cheques. Cheques came to a hundred and ten, credit cards to three forty, so he's only got about four hundred in cash. Hardly worth the trouble, really.'

'And did he take it all from a safe?'

'No,' Chris said, feeling embarrassed. 'We keep it in a filing cabinet.'

The two policemen looked at each other. 'A filing cabinet?' they both said at the same time.

'My boss is too tight to buy a safe. Maybe he will now.'

'And do you have Mr Blake's address?'

Chris handed over a piece of paper.

'Okay. We'll get someone to drive over and see if he's still there. We'll give you a ring later.'

'Will that be today?'

'Hopefully.'

Then the two policemen ambled out.

Chris busied himself with filling shelves and dusting bottles, and serving the few customers that came in. He wondered whether the police would find Hugh or not, or whether he really cared that much anyway. Several hours later, the one person he didn't want to see opened the door and stepped inside.

'Morning, Rowan,' he said, without enthusiasm.

'Morning, Chris. How are things?' Rowan wasn't even looking at him. He was already heading for some bins of South African red that had come in last week.

'Do you want the bad news first or the good news?' Chris said.

That made Rowan look up. 'I don't want any bad news so give me the good first.'

'Well, you remember that guy I hired to work Sundays? Hugh Blake?'

'Yeah?'

'Well, a customer who comes in on Sundays – and just happens to be a security guard at Marks & Spencer – has been watching him for a few weeks and noticing that he doesn't always ring sales into the till.'

'Oh yeah?'

'Which I always take to mean he's nicking money.'

'Absolutely.'

'So I gave him the sack on Sunday and worked that day myself.'

Chris paused, and watched Rowan nod his head. 'And that was the good news?'

'It doesn't get any better. I came in today and found Sunday's takings missing. The bastard had a spare set of keys cut and came back yesterday. He took the whole paper bag from the filing cabinet. We've lost eight hundred and fifty-two quid.'

Chris watched as Rowan's face slowly turned red. 'Well, that's a fucking disaster.'

'So I called the police and they've gone to check him out. I'm waiting for them to ring back.'

Rowan seemed to wobble a bit on his feet so Chris fetched the till stool and brought it up behind him. 'Are you all right?' he asked, guiding Rowan on to the stool.

Rowan's breathing came in short, sharp bursts and Chris hoped he wasn't about to have a heart attack. He walked quickly into the storeroom and came back with a glass of water. He handed it to Rowan, who sipped it quietly.

Then the telephone rang and Chris walked over to the till. It was the police. While he spoke to them, Rowan looked at him. Chris put the phone down. 'He's done a runner. Left his flat yesterday.'

'Jesus fucking Christ,' Rowan said quietly, then drank some more water.

They sat in silence for a few minutes and then Rowan said, 'I want that money back, Chris. I don't know how to do that right now, but I can't afford to lose that much. I'll have to hold you responsible for it.'

'How do you mean?'

'I mean paying me back. Maybe a little each month off your wages.'

'That would take forever. Aren't you insured against such a thing?'

Rowan shook his head. 'Because I haven't got a safe, I can't claim.'

Chris nodded. He might have guessed. He didn't bother mentioning the times he'd tried persuading Rowan to get one. He sat there wondering when the next mini-disaster was going to strike. First his window falling in and now this. If Rowan wanted the money back that would mean he'd have to hand over the remaining five hundred pounds in his savings, plus his share of the blackjack winnings, and that still wouldn't be enough. He would be cleaned out completely, except for his original five hundred in the blackjack kitty. What a disastrous week this was turning out to be.

'You may think that's unfair,' Rowan said, 'but you did hire the guy. Didn't you check his references?'

'No, not until last week. He got fired from his last job as well.'

'I prove my point. You really must be more careful about

these things. And all because you wanted to go out with a young piece of fluff. How did that turn out anyway?'

'It didn't turn out. She was already going out with someone else.'

Rowan shook his head. 'That's bad judgement. Twice. And it's going to cost you eight hundred and fifty quid. I presume Saturday's takings went in the nightsafe?'

'Yeah, as per usual,' Chris said. They only had one night-safe wallet, so Saturday's takings went straight into the bank over the road while Sunday's stayed in the shop. Another problem that should've been sorted out a long time ago. Chris couldn't bear to look at Rowan and his self-satisfied face. All of a sudden he was seeing him in a new light; like the real miser he'd always suspected him to be.

Eventually, Rowan stood up, put the glass of water on the stool, and picked out six bottles of wine. Chris put them in two bags and they mumbled goodbye, hardly looking at each other. On his way out of the door, Rowan accidentally knocked the stool with his walking stick and the glass of water fell to the floor and smashed. He apologised and Chris ushered him out. He was glad when he finally had the place to himself.

He spent the rest of the day in a foul mood, mentally trying to work out his finances, in case he felt like walking out of his job for the way Rowan was treating him. He would ask Brad tonight – they were playing cards again without Edie – how much his cut of their stake was worth so far. It wouldn't be much. Maybe they would win thousands tonight and his problem would be solved.

At four o'clock, he walked into the back room and opened a bottle of white wine. He always kept some chilled in the fridge for visiting sales reps. He sat at the desk, looked out through the one-way glass, and sipped away. His life had reached another low, and once again he would have to climb right back out of the hole.

31

FOR ONCE IN his life, Dave Brill had come down to the ground, and was having lunch with Luke. They were sitting in the driveway of a semi-detached on a plank of wood, leaning against the wall. Brill had a London A-Z in front of him and was flicking through the index. It was Wednesday afternoon and he was trying to plan the next move on Chris Small.

'It had an animal's name in it,' he said to Luke. 'Can't you think of any streets with animal's names in them?'

'What, like Pig Street, or Donkey Street?' Luke laughed.

Brill looked at him. 'Yeah, that sort of thing. Except probably a bit more subtle.'

'You've got to be joking,' Luke scoffed. 'Do you know how many streets there are in London?'

'Yeah, but there can't be many with animals' names in them.' But Luke just ignored him, munching away on his cheese and salad cream sandwich.

It was yesterday that Brill had the brainwave. He remembered a conversation with Rosetta, one they'd had when they were in All Bar One in Bromley. She had just had her first meeting with Small and he had told her he worked in an off-licence in London, and he'd mentioned the street. All Brill could remember now was that the street had an animal's name in it. He ran his finger down through the index, knowing he would find it eventually.

It was a fine sunny day and the chimney they were working on was going well. They would be finished tomorrow and then Brill could look forward to Friday off and a long weekend, albeit a long weekend with Evelyn and the kids. Normally he would have spent that Friday round at Rosetta's, bonking his brains out, but things would have to revert to normal for a while. He could always try thinking of Rosetta while he was on top of Evelyn, but that would take some imagination; she was about three stone heavier.

Two sandwiches later Luke looked at him and said, 'Lamb. Does it have lamb in it?'

Brill looked at his sandwich. 'Chicken,' he said. 'Who the hell has lamb in a sandwich?'

'The street,' Luke said. 'Does the street name have a lamb in it?'

Brill hurriedly turned to the Ls and there it was. 'Lambs Conduit Street. That's it! How could I have forgotten? It's got a conduit in it as well. And me a fucking builder.' He shook his head.

'I remembered because there's a nice boozer there called The Lamb. One of those old boozers with a nice atmosphere.'

'You did well, Luke,' Brill said sarcastically. 'I was already on the Js. You saved me about two minutes of searching.'

Luke looked at him. 'Fucking gratitude, that is.'

Brill laughed and patted him on the back. 'Now what we have to do is work out our next move. Maybe you could go there after work and find out which off-licence it is. There can't be many.'

'Will do. It's not that far from where I live. About a twenty-minute walk.'

'Great.'

'And then I'll plan a little surprise for him.'

'That's my boy. You'll be rich when this is all over.'

Luke licked his lips. 'A thousand pounds!'

At five o'clock, Luke was walking up and down Lambs Conduit Street. He could only see one off-licence – Rowan's – so that must be the one. He decided to walk in and buy some beer.

He recognised Chris Small as soon as he stepped inside, from the description that Dave had given him. George

Clooney, he'd said. George Clooney without the money or the taste in clothes. He was sitting at the till, reading a newspaper. He looked up and Luke nodded at him. Small nodded back.

Luke wandered around, looking at bottles of beer on the shelves and cans stacked on the floor, but there were so many available these days it was hard to make a choice. He looked over the centre stack at Small and asked, 'Are there any beers you would recommend?'

Small looked up at him and said, 'What sort of beer do you drink?'

Luke shrugged. 'The wet kind.'

Small laughed. 'Bottled beer, canned? Lager, bitter, American, European, dark or light?'

Luke was getting confused. 'Just something that slips down nice and easy.'

Then he watched as Small got off his stool and came over. He stood right next to him and Luke looked down at him. This was all very useful. It was handy knowing someone's exact height before picking a fight. Some guys, when they climbed off a stool or got out of a seat, were bigger than you expected. He reckoned Small was about five foot ten.

'Well, I've tasted most of these,' Small said, 'and a lot of them, you can't tell the difference between. But do you prefer a bottle or a can?'

'Can,' Luke said quickly.

'Okay. Try this one. I've always liked it.'

Small held up a silver can with a name beginning with G. Luke looked at it and couldn't begin to see how to pronounce it.

'It's called Grolsch. From…' He watched Small look at the can. 'Well, it doesn't say where it's from. Brewed in the UK, it says here in small print. Probably Dutch originally. Anyway, who cares? It goes down easy and has a nice kick.'

'Good,' Luke said. 'That'll do. I'll take four.'

'Would you like some chilled ones?'

'Yeah, okay.'

He watched while Small went to a fridge and lifted out a four-pack. Then he went to the till and put them in a bag.

Luke walked over and dipped into his dirty jeans for some money.

'That'll be three pounds eighty please.'

'Fucking hell,' Luke said.

'Cheaper than the pub,' Small said, smiling at him.

'I suppose so,' Luke said. Then he got his change, said 'thank you' and walked out.

He cracked open a can and swigged as he walked. Small didn't seem such a bad bloke really, but thoughts like that would have to be banished from his head. He would have to focus on something negative about him so that he could go into the job without any emotion. He thought about how Small had nicked Dave's girlfriend, Rosetta. He would focus on that. That was something bad he'd done. That would get him in the mood.

There had been plenty of blokes in the past he'd had fights with who he'd hated at the time, but then later when he'd seen them again, they'd shared a drink or two and got on like old friends. It was just par for the course. After all, that's what happened with boxers. They hated each other before a fight, but were best buddies, in each other's arms, by the end of it. Luke didn't know why. It wasn't some kind of queer thing. More like kindred spirits coming together. He swigged his beer and smiled. And people said he wasn't a deep thinker!

He reached home in no time and walked into the piss, smelling lobby. Then up in the lift to the fifth floor. When he walked in he found a note from his mother on the kitchen counter. 'Just gone to the theatre. Supper in the fridge.' That suited Luke down to the ground. He could drink his beer in peace tonight and there was a live cup match on Sky later. What could be more perfect?

He could also think about his plan of attack on Chris Small.

32

CHRIS WAS SITTING in the off-licence on Friday when he got a phone call from Brad.

'We got the all clear,' he said.

'Great!' Chris said. 'How did she take it?'

'She was okay about it. She said you should never disrupt a winning run. She'll wait until we lose badly and then she'll come back in.'

'That's very sporting of her. I didn't think she'd take it so well.'

'Edie is always the ultimate professional. She knows that anything we make goes into the pot. We're making money for her while she sits at home, watching TV.'

'She's not dumb,' Chris agreed.

He hung up and couldn't wait for the day to be over. On Tuesday, their second evening in the casinos together, he and Brad had won nearly two hundred and fifty pounds. They had visited two casinos, and either Brad's counting was a lot better than Edie's, or they just worked better together as a team.

Chris had been extremely relaxed that evening, thanks to the bottle of white he'd consumed at work after his troublesome day, but he'd stayed off the booze while they were playing and had won some big hands. In the first casino, they had made a quick exit when a pit boss came over and really gave them the eye. Chris had been sitting there nervously, wondering if he would get the fateful tap on the shoulder. Apparently, that was the worst thing that could happen. He would be put on a blacklist and barred from every casino in London. That was definitely to be avoided when he was trying to earn back Rowan's eight hundred and fifty pounds.

In the second casino, they had won heavily again, then

gone for a drink and headed home. Chris was looking forward to seeing the new balance sheet tonight.

At eight o'clock he shut the shop and went to meet Brad in The Angel. He walked in and saw him sitting at a table, drinking a Coke. He waved, walked to the bar, and bought one himself.

When he sat down he said, 'They probably think we're a couple of poofs, sitting here drinking Cokes together.'

'Poofs?'

'Sorry. Gays. You Americans. Soon we'll all be so PC and polite we won't be able to say a thing.'

'And being PC came from America?'

'Everything else does. Why should that be so different? Let me see the balance sheet.'

Brad reached into a jacket pocket and brought out the latest computer printout. Chris was pleased to see the profit now stood at £860. Divided three ways though that was still only about £280 for him. Still a long way to go but at least it was heading in the right direction.

'Disappointed?' Brad asked.

Chris shook his head. 'No, it's just a long way from that eight hundred and fifty I owe my boss.'

'We'll be there sooner than you think. The way you and I are going we'll soon be millionaires.'

'Yeah, right.'

'Just be patient. That's the hallmark of every decent gambler.'

Chris nodded. Being patient was not what he was into right now. He had lost all interest in the off-licence since Rowan's treatment of him on Tuesday, and had decided to leave when the eight hundred and fifty pounds was all paid back.

They finished their drinks and decided to catch a bus to The Albert casino on Edgware Road. It was a cool night with rain in the air, a stiff breeze starting to blow. They entered the Albert separately and went through their usual routine.

One and a half hours later, Chris walked out after stopping for a quick beer at the bar. Brad had already left and he found him in their usual bus shelter. It had been raining while they were inside and there weren't many people around, even though it was Friday night. They did a high-five to celebrate yet another good night together.

'How much did you get?' Brad asked.

'A hundred and seventy-five. How about you?'

'About seventy-five. Another good night's work.'

'We keep this up and Edie will never get back in!'

They both laughed and started walking towards the bus stop they needed on Oxford Street, the wind and a fine rain blowing in their faces. When they got there they turned their backs to the rain.

'Why doesn't this stop have a shelter?' Brad cursed.

'Because it's ours,' Chris said. He looked across the street and saw a man on the other side of the road he recognised, but couldn't recall from where. He was tall and skinny with an untidy beard. Then he watched as the man crossed the road towards them. He was carrying a long sack of some kind, like the kind you put tent poles in. Chris couldn't figure out why someone would be carrying a tent pole bag down Oxford Street. The man stopped on an island in the middle of the road and waited.

Chris nudged Brad. 'Weirdo on the horizon.'

Brad looked to where Chris was looking. 'Yeah. London's full of them.'

The man stepped into the road and started towards them. He still looked familiar, but then Chris got worried when he saw the tent bag drop to reveal a baseball bat in the man's right hand. Then the man headed straight for them, raised the bat and swung it at Chris's head.

Chris had always had pretty good reactions and he ducked as the bat went over him. The blow hit Brad instead though, smack on the head, and he heard a terrible crack. Then the man was running down the road, taking the baseball bat with him.

Chris bent down to Brad who was now lying on the pavement, a dazed look on his face. There was blood coming from a cut on his forehead, smeared by the rain. Chris looked up for help and was relieved to see three people running towards them. When they reached him, he said, 'Has anyone got a mobile?' All three produced one from their pockets.

Luke was running for his life. He darted down a side street and in a panic threw the baseball bat into a pile of black rubbish-bags. Then he carried on running.

He kept to the side streets and started walking when he was out of breath. It was only another ten minutes to the Gillhead flats and he walked indoors looking like a drowned rat.

Thankfully, his mother was at another show, so he stripped off his wet clothes and hung them over the radiators. Then he ran a hot bath, grabbed a can of Grolsch from the fridge, and took it to the bathroom.

He started to relax as the beer took effect and thought everything through that had just happened. He had just made a complete balls-up of the whole thing. He had hit the man standing next to Chris Small, the friend of his he'd seen him with earlier in the evening, going into the casino. He hadn't reckoned on Small ducking; most people would just freeze in that situation. He wondered how badly he'd hurt the other man.

After half an hour he climbed out of the bath, dried off and went straight to his bedroom. He pulled on boxer shorts and a T-shirt and climbed into bed. He lay there shivering, as if he had a fever. And then he started worrying about the baseball bat. Why the fuck had he thrown it away? If the police found it his prints would be all over it. And he'd be on record because of that time he beat up the ticket inspector. He'd better get up early in the morning and see if it was still there. He closed his eyes and tried to sleep. He wished his mother were there so the flat didn't feel so empty.

33

CHRIS WAITED IN a corridor at Charing Cross hospital for Edie. He had rung her as soon as Brad had been wheeled away but it was so late in the evening, he wondered how she would get there from Orpington. She might have missed the last train. It had taken the ambulance twenty-five minutes to get to the scene and Chris wondered if that time delay would turn out to be crucial. He had covered Brad with his coat, then sat shivering in the rain while a crowd of people gathered and offered comfort. Another put his coat under Brad's head and all they could do was sit and wait. It was the longest twenty-five minutes of Chris's life.

At the hospital a policeman took Chris aside and asked questions. Chris knew very well that the attack was something to do with Dave Brill but he wasn't going to tell the police that just yet. He wanted to have a word or two with Brill first, then tell the police all he knew and let them finish the job. So he stood in front of the policeman and shook his head; no officer, I don't know of any reason why this happened.

Just after midnight, Chris turned and saw Edie walking towards him. He stood and waited, and gave her a hug. He told her all he knew about Brad's condition – which wasn't good – and then they sat down together.

'Maybe this wouldn't have happened if I was with you,' Edie said. 'Maybe it was someone from the casino who spotted you card counting. Or a mugger who saw you coming out.'

'Don't blame yourself,' Chris said. 'That'll get you nowhere.' He wasn't going to tell her about Dave Brill either. The last thing he needed right now was for her to blame him for things. He took hold of her hand. 'Maybe it was just a mugger. God knows, there's enough of them around.'

They sat together for another few hours. There was still no improvement and eventually they let them into the ward to sit by Brad's bed. He had various tubes going into his arms and nose, and was still unconscious. Chris decided there was no point in hanging around. He would go to the shop and see if he could get some sleep. He said goodbye to Edie and left her at Brad's side.

He walked out into the deserted streets. He felt incredibly depressed and angry. He would ring Rosetta during the day and find out Dave Brill's address. Then he would pay him a visit.

When he got to the shop he turned the alarm off quickly and went into the back room. He had never slept in the shop before but had slept in other shops in the past. It was never a pleasant experience but it was better than sitting up all night in the hospital. He turned on the electric fan heater, then flattened some cardboard boxes and spread them on the concrete floor for his bed. He found some sheets of bubble wrap and made them in to a pillow, then took off his shoes. He turned off the light and lay down under his coat leaving the heater on automatic cut off.

Almost as soon as he'd laid down, he remembered where he'd seen the attacker before. He was that tall, weird-looking guy who'd come into the off-licence a few days ago, asking about beer. Chris had sold him four cans of Grolsch. Maybe he'd hated the Grolsch and come to pay him back. But the more he thought about it, the more he was certain it was something to do with Dave Brill. This was obviously the guy Brill had paid to do him in. The builder Rosetta had talked about. Maybe Brill had seen the hole in the wall of his house, seen that he'd moved on, and changed the plan of attack to where he worked. Only the attacker hadn't caught him at work but waited until later in the evening. He had obviously followed him from the shop into the West End. But how had they known where he worked? Then he remembered he had told Rosetta, back when she was still in cahoots with Brill. It was all starting to fit together.

It was after three o'clock now and he stared up at the ceiling. The orange glow from the streetlights almost made it cosy but he knew it would be an uncomfortable night with a few hours of sleep snatched here and there. He closed his eyes and hoped that Brad would be all right.

When light started seeping through the windows of Luke Tremble's room, he climbed out of bed and got dressed. He grabbed his coat from the hooks by the front door and sneaked out quietly.

He walked quickly back down the route he'd taken last night. He still felt sleepy from a night of uncomfortable dreams. In one of them, he'd dreamt that two cops had come to pick him up, holding the baseball bat in front of them. They'd dangled it under his nose and it had been white with fingerprint dust. They said he was going down for life. Then he had been pushed into a cell but the cell had turned into a lift shaft, and he'd gone screaming and falling towards the bottom. Luckily, he'd woken up before he landed.

The street he'd dropped the baseball bat in was just off Oxford Street, either Duke or Orchard, he couldn't remember exactly. He walked down both streets looking for the rubbish sacks but both streets were completely clean. Had the rubbish men been there already? If they had then that was just as good. They would have thrown the bat into the back of their van along with all the other crap.

Luke started to breathe a little easier, but he would still have preferred the bat to be safely in his hands. He carried on walking to Charing Cross, then caught the train to Elmhurst.

At the station, he rang Dave Brill.

'How did it go?' Brill asked, sleepily.

'Not too good,' Luke said. 'I'll tell you when I see you.'

'What do you mean, when you see me? It's Saturday.'

Luke wondered if he'd heard right but then realised his mistake. 'Shit. I forgot. I thought it was another working day.'

'Pull yourself together,' Brill said. 'I'll come and get you.'

Luke stood outside the station, reading the *Sun*, looking to see if there was any report of the attack. There wasn't.

When Brill turned up in the Toyota Hiace, Luke jumped into the passenger seat and shut the door.

'Spill the beans,' Brill said, then listened while Luke told his story. At the end of it he said, 'Fucking hell,' then slipped into silence.

Luke sat there waiting for something to happen. Nothing did. He cleared his throat. 'That's me out of it, Dave. I don't care about the money, you can keep it. I'll just be glad to get out of this without getting banged up.'

Brill nodded. 'Fair enough. I'd better finish the job myself.'

Luke didn't want to know any details. He opened the passenger door. 'Well, I guess I'd better catch the train home again.'

'Have you had breakfast yet?' Brill asked.

'No.'

'Well let me buy you some. At least make your journey worthwhile.'

'Yeah, okay,' Luke said. 'Thanks.' He shut the passenger door and slid down in the seat.

34

CHRIS MANAGED TO have a lie-in on Saturday morning because he didn't have too far to go to work. About five feet to be precise. But having a lie-in on some flattened cardboard wasn't exactly luxurious. When he did get up, at half-past nine, his back and neck were both stiff. He went into the toilet and splashed water on his face at the sink. Then he walked outside to the Indian supermarket and bought a newspaper and some apple turnovers for breakfast.

When he was back in the shop he rang the hospital and asked about Brad. The nurse wasn't very helpful, and all she could tell him was that Brad was still unconscious. Chris thanked her and felt very worried. He wondered if Edie was still there and if she'd rung Brad's parents yet. She really ought to get them over from America straight away.

He opened the shop at ten and ate the cakes at the till with a cup of tea. He scoured the newspaper for any news of the attack but it didn't get a mention. It would only get a mention if Brad died and Chris didn't want to think about that scenario. He turned to the sports pages and immersed himself in those, instead.

It was a long, slow day and Chris decided that tomorrow would be his final one in the off-licence. Last night's attack had made him realise that life was too short to spend working for people who didn't appreciate him. It would land him in the shit financially but he would worry about that later. He would probably have enough to last a month or so, which would hopefully be enough time to find another job. He realised he was having a knee-jerk reaction to the situation, but that was the only way he knew of bringing about change. Too often in the past he would let things drift and he was too old to let that happen any more. A knee-jerk was the best way to kick-start a stagnant life.

In the afternoon, he rang Rosetta and told her what had happened.

'What a bastard that man is,' she said, when he'd finished. 'How on earth did I manage to keep going out with him?'

'You tell me,' Chris said. 'I guess they got my work address from you.'

The line went silent for a while. 'What do you mean?'

'Back when you were on Brill's side, did you tell him my work address?'

Rosetta was silent again and then said, 'I suppose I did. Sorry. It must have been that meeting we had in All Bar One. When you walked in and saw us both.'

'That's exactly what I thought. Well, at least I know it was them. Now what I need from you is Dave Brill's address.'

'And why do you need that?'

'I'm going to pay him a little visit tonight.'

'And do what?'

'I haven't decided yet.'

'Do you think that's wise?'

'Is anything wise?'

He could hear Rosetta taking a deep breath. 'I don't want anything bad happening to you, Chris. I'm starting to get fond of you. And your body.'

Chris chuckled. 'Maybe I'll just sail a brick through his window or something.'

'Don't do that, he's got a couple of kids. You might hit one of them. If you want to hit his weak spot, go for his BMW. He's madly in love with that.'

'That sounds like a very good idea. Thanks for the tip.'

'Am I going to see you this weekend?'

'Probably. How about Sunday evening? Come round about half-nine.'

'Sunday would be perfect.'

'But I still need his address.' He grabbed a pen while she gave him directions.

They hung up and Chris sat and thought some more. A
BMW. He had never trashed a car before. It might be quite
good fun. But he would have to do it quickly and quietly. No
doubt all kinds of car alarms would go off. He tried to figure
out how to do it.

Instead of catching a train to Elmhurst after work, Chris
caught one to Sidcup. He could walk to Dave Brill's house
from there and then catch a bus home. He had already decided
what he was going to do to Brill's car, and it would be silent
and effective.

It was no problem finding the house, a three-bedroom
detached in a semi-circular road. There was a Toyota Hiace
and a BMW parked in the drive, the BMW behind the Toyota,
both of them reversed in. Chris had been worried on the way
down that the BMW might be locked in a garage, which would
have scuppered his plans straight away. But luck was on his
side. There it was, all shiny and black, ready and waiting for
him, looking more like a tank than a car.

He walked on to the driveway like he owned the house,
with a small screwdriver he'd taken from work in his left hand.
He scratched the whole of the left side of the paintwork as he
walked towards the back wheel, and then knelt down. He
unscrewed the air cap on the wheel and started letting out the
air. He knew he had to be careful because any sudden move-
ment of the car would probably set off the alarm, depending
on how sensitive it was. When the tyre was half flat, he walked
around the back to the other rear wheel. He let out half the air
on that one as well and then walked towards the front wheel,
scratching the paintwork on the driver's side as he passed.

The street was well lit, and Chris knew that if anyone
looked out of a window they would see him, but that was a
risk worth taking. He reckoned most people would be flaked
out in front of the TV at this time of the evening anyway, and
if Brill came out he would just face him here and now. He was
in a bad enough mood to give him a good sock on the jaw.

After the third tyre was done, Chris walked around the front end of the BMW to the fourth. When that was finished, it meant all tyres were halfway down. All he had to do now was to start at the back again and let them all the way down. Then he could disappear.

As he started on the back wheel for the second time, though, the BMW shuddered slightly and the alarm went off. A loud, screeching noise filled the air and Chris stood up and walked down the side of the garage. He had planned before-hand that this was a wiser move than walking off down the street. He stood in the dark, between the garage and a wire fence, then heard doors opening and feet approaching the BMW. A car door opened and then the alarm fell silent.

Chris listened and a voice said, 'Fucking hell!'

There was silence and then a woman came outside and Brill was talking to her. Chris couldn't make out all their words but Brill was not a happy man. He couldn't help but smile. He looked into the back garden to see if there was any way out but there wasn't. He would have to wait until things calmed down at the front and then walk away. He crouched down in the cold and waited.

Later in the evening, Dave Brill paced his back garden and rang Rosetta on his mobile. He had a glass of whisky in his other hand. When Rosetta answered, he said aggressively, 'This is your ex-lover boy. How are you?'

'Fine,' Rosetta said. 'And how are you?'

'Extremely pissed-off,' Brill said, trying to keep his emotions under control. 'Someone just let the air out of my BMW tyres and scratched the paintwork on both sides.'

'Sorry to hear that,' Rosetta said in a flat voice. 'It was probably kids.'

'I doubt if it's kids. More like your new lover boy.'

'Excuse me? Are you drunk?'

'Not nearly as drunk as I should be.'

'Look, Dave. I was just going to bed. I really don't care

about your precious BMW and what some kids have done to it.'

'I want to know where Small is living,' Brill said quickly, before she had a chance to hang up.

'Now why should I tell you that?'

'Because he's the one that did it and I want to beat the shit out of him.'

'Big words from a big boy. Why don't you just grow up?'

He didn't have an answer to that one. He stood staring at his neat lawn, the tidy flower beds all looked after by Evelyn, the back fence and the back of the house opposite. It was a serene view but that was hardly how he felt. He took the mobile away from his left ear and turned it off. He wouldn't bother calling Rosetta again. She was lost to him. He would think of another way of finding Small and finish the job himself. He slugged the whisky back in one and went indoors.

35

WHEN CHRIS WOKE up on Sunday morning, his first sleepy thought was that he had a nice day off to look forward to. Then he remembered that he had to go to work, his final day at the off-licence. He climbed out of bed and went to the shower room.

He ate breakfast in the canteen with about twenty others, but once again sat on his own. He wondered how long he could stay in the YMCA this second time before it drove him crazy. Then he realised he would have to stay until he found a job, because no one would rent a place to him unless he was employed. Things were looking bleaker by the minute.

He made the long walk to the station then caught the train to Charing Cross. When he got to work he rang Rowan, but he wasn't at home. He left a message on his answer machine, saying he would be leaving at the end of the day. He told him he didn't think much of the way he was being treated.

After he'd hung up he started to work out his finances. He reckoned Rowan owed him about two weeks' wages, which came to £696. If he left a cheque for £154, then that would be the £850 all paid back. Seen in these simple terms, Chris wondered why he'd been so worried about leaving, these past few days. Together with the deposit on his flat, plus his share of blackjack money, plus his five hundred still in the building society, he would have more than enough to tide him over until he found another job. He wrote a note to Rowan, explaining his actions, adding sarcastically that he hoped he would find someone more suited to the job quickly. Then he waited for the day to end.

It was a busy Sunday and thankfully the hours passed quickly, but Chris decided to shut an hour early just for the hell of it. The takings were over nine hundred pounds, and he left it all in the filing cabinet for Rowan to count himself. The shop would be shut tomorrow and that would give Rowan enough time to organise things for re-opening on Tuesday. Maybe he would even have to come in and work some hours himself. It would probably do him good. Get him off his bony backside.

Chris collected all his belongings from around the shop: a few cassettes and books, a couple of mugs. He put them all in a carrier, set the alarm, and locked the front door for the last time. Then he posted the keys back through the letterbox.

On the walk to Charing Cross, instead of feeling elated, Chris started feeling depressed. Once again he was back in the land of the unemployed, a place he didn't like lingering in for too long. He wondered whether to go to the hospital to see Brad but he didn't have the energy. Instead, on a whim, he veered towards Shaftesbury Avenue. He had a sudden urge to gamble.

He had a choice of three casinos in the area and decided to visit Lester's in Archer Street. He had been there several times with Edie and liked the fake stone walls, the feeling of being inside a cave. He checked in at reception and handed over his coat and bag.

He walked into the smoky atmosphere, took a seat at a blackjack table and handed over fifty pounds. There were three other people at the table, but he took no notice of their banter, concentrating hard on his cards instead. Within ten minutes he had doubled his money.

Chris felt his pulse quicken. Was tonight going to be one of those nights when all the cards fell his way? He started doubling his bets to ten pounds a hand.

He lost a couple of hands very quickly but soon got back in his stride with a blackjack, a successful double down, and a heavy win on a pair of split nines. He reckoned he was now about two hundred pounds ahead. He sensed the others at the table getting quiet, watching his every move.

He glanced up and noticed a floor manager looking at him

from his high seat next to the table. He was a big man with a black beard, overweight and unfriendly looking. Chris purposely lost a couple of hands and then cut back to five pounds a hand. He won one and lost one, picked up his chips and left the table.

He cashed in at the window at the back, and almost licked his lips when he saw two hundred and twenty pounds coming his way. He gave the cashier a big smile but she just ignored him. He stuffed the money in his jeans and went to reception to pick up his things.

On the walk to Charing Cross, Chris felt on cloud nine. He had just had his biggest ever winnings on his own, and he'd only been in there for about forty-five minutes. Maybe he was starting to get the hang of things. Maybe this was what he was cut out to do. Then he dismissed the thought as foolishness. He told himself to get his feet back on the ground. But still, he couldn't wait to tell Edie and Brad.

When he reached the station there was a train already waiting and he stepped right on. Thirty minutes later, he was getting off at Elmhurst.

He saw a figure sitting on a platform bench and realised it was Edie. She looked up and saw him, stood and walked towards him. From the look on her face he knew something was wrong, and then she came straight into his arms and started crying on his shoulder. He held her until she calmed down.

'What's wrong?' he asked, although he was pretty sure he knew.

She still had her head on his shoulder as she mumbled, 'Brad died this morning.'

'Oh shit,' was all Chris could say, then he led her back to the bench where they both sat down.

When they'd recovered, they made the long walk up the hill and along the road to the YMCA. Brad had died in the morning, never regaining consciousness, and his parents had arrived too late in the afternoon. Edie had stayed with them a while and then walked around the West End in a daze. Eventually she had made it to Charing Cross, intending to get the train home, but had got off at Elmhurst instead to wait for Chris.

They held hands as they walked and, despite all that had happened, Chris felt good having her by his side. He wondered what would happen when they got back to the YMCA. Did Edie want to stay the night? Did she want to sleep with him? He had read somewhere that a bereavement could make a person randy, and had experienced it first-hand a long time ago in his twenties. An old girlfriend had just been to the funeral of her grandmother and, on turning up at Chris's crummy bedsit, had almost torn his clothes off. He wondered if this was going to be another of those times. He felt guilty thinking such things but they kept entering his head. Hopefully they would just talk and spend the evening together, then go to sleep without any physical contact. He felt so sad at the moment he didn't think he could respond to sexual advances anyway.

'So this is where you're living now?' Edie said, as they walked down the driveway of the YMCA.

'Yeah, it's like a second home. I lived here for a couple of years once, but that's another story.'

'I'd like to hear it someday.'

'Okay,' Chris said. He felt instantly better. Edie's words hinted that she would like to see him again.

They were still holding hands when they reached the front door. 'You'd better let go of me,' Chris said. 'Physical contact is frowned upon in here.'

He was pulling open the front door when he heard a car in the driveway behind them. He turned to look but the lights blinded his eyes. Then he followed Edie into the building.

When Rosetta got home she climbed out of her car and slammed the door. She kept muttering to herself 'two-timing bastard' as she walked up the drive and opened the front door.

She turned on the hall lights and went into the living room.

She fixed herself a gin and tonic and sat in the dark, cursing. She had been looking forward to this evening and now everything was ruined. She hadn't seen Chris for six days but obviously he didn't need long to find someone new. She picked up the phone and dialed a number.

'Hello?'

'It's me,' she said. 'Do you still want to know where Chris Small is living?'

'Yeah! Too right I do. Where is he?'

For a second Rosetta wondered if she was doing the right thing, but then she thought, Sod it, all men were bastards, they deserved what they got. 'He's at the Elmhurst YMCA, room 205.'

'Hey, that's great,' Dave Brill said. 'Why the sudden change of mind?'

'Don't ask,' Rosetta said, and then she cut him off. She didn't want to speak to him or any other man for a long time. She went to the liquor cabinet and strengthened her drink.

36

IN CHRIS'S ROOM, Edie talked and cried. She reminisced about her time with Brad, and Chris had to go down the hall to the toilet for a wad of paper to dry her tears. Then he sat in the armchair and listened, while Edie lay on the bed, getting it all off her chest.

They had been there an hour when there was a soft knock at the door. Chris suddenly remembered that Rosetta was meant to be coming round. He walked to the door and opened it, but instead of Rosetta, Dave Brill came bursting through, pushing Chris back into the room on to his desk.

'Fuck around with my car, would you?' Brill said, reaching for Chris's throat.

Chris reached for the only weapon to hand, his laptop computer. As Brill tightened his grip he swung it round and whacked him on the side of his head. Brill looked dazed for a second and then dropped to the floor. Chris put the computer down and shut the door.

Edie was now standing up, looking shaken. 'What was that all about?'

'This bastard has been hassling me for weeks,' Chris said. 'I'll tell you about it later. Help me lift him up.'

They struggled to lift his weight into the plastic chair, then Chris went to the wardrobe and brought out a roll of brown packing tape. He put Brill's arms behind his back and taped his wrists together. Then he taped his ankles.

'What are you going to do with him?' Edie asked.

'Just teach him a lesson,' Chris said. 'I won't harm him.' He stood looking at Brill, wondering what to do next. 'Can we stay at your place tonight?'

'Of course,' Edie said.

'And a few more nights as well?'

'I don't see why not. I don't know how we're going to get there though.'

'If you go down to the lobby there's some minicab numbers next to the phone box. Get one to come here in about fifteen minutes. Wait for me downstairs.'

'Okay.'

Chris let Edie out of the room and started packing his things together. He put all his clothes back in his two suitcases and his other stuff in the cardboard box. Finally, he put the laptop in, wondering if it would ever work again.

He was still wondering what to do with Brill when he spotted a mobile phone attached to his belt. He quickly unclipped it then forced Brill's mouth open. He stuffed the mobile in lengthways, then wound some brown tape around his head to keep it firmly locked in.

Brill opened his eyes and looked at Chris. Chris slapped him around the face then grabbed him by the neck.

'My friend just died today because of you. Now I'm going to leave you here all night and then I'm going to ring the police and get them to pick you up in the morning. Meanwhile, enjoy your mobile.'

Chris picked up his two suitcases and put them in the hall. Then he did the same with the cardboard box. As he left the room, Brill started struggling. Chris turned the light off and locked the door behind him.

When the taxi came they loaded Chris's things into the boot and drove away. He had left his keys at reception, saying he wasn't coming back. He didn't owe them any rent.

It didn't take long to get to Orpington, and they unloaded his things and carried them into the flat. Chris searched through his box for the business card Brill had given him, when he'd first come knocking at his door. If he remembered correctly it had his mobile number on it.

'Can I borrow your phone?' Chris asked.

'Yes,' Edie said. 'Who are you ringing?'

'That guy I just tied up.'

Chris looked at the card and dialed the number. He listened to it ringing and then an answer service came on. He put the telephone back down.

'Did you notice he had a mobile?' he said. 'I'll ring him a few times during the night. Hopefully, the tune will drive him crazy.'

Edie looked at him warily. 'I think I'm missing something. Maybe you'd better tell me everything that's been going on.'

They stayed up until two in the morning and Chris told Edie everything, leaving nothing out. It would've been easier to lie but he wanted her to know the whole truth. They drank some whisky and ate some stale cake. The only part he couldn't figure was how Brill had found out he was staying at the YMCA. Then Edie went to her bedroom while Chris slept on the sofa.

He slept badly and when seven o'clock came around he rang the police in Elmhurst. 'There's a man locked up in room 205 of the YMCA, who's responsible for a murder,' he told them. 'His name is Dave Brill.'

The policeman took some notes and told Chris he would have to come down to the station and make a statement. Chris said he would come down in the afternoon.

He went back to the sofa and dozed until Edie woke up. She came into the room, dressed in pyjamas and dressing gown. Chris watched as she walked to the windows and drew the curtains. He thought she looked wonderful. Then she knelt on the floor in front of him.

'I've been thinking throughout the night,' she said. 'I didn't get much sleep and I really think we should part company.'

Chris couldn't believe what he was hearing. He thought they'd got on really well last night. 'You'd better tell me why,' he said.

Edie looked at the floor. 'It's Brad, I guess. He was killed because of something you were mixed up in and I'll be thinking of that whenever we're together. I think it's best if we go our separate ways. It was good fun while it lasted. I'm not going to play blackjack any more. I'm going to quit my job and do something else.'

Chris nodded. Maybe Edie was right. Maybe their relationship had been doomed from the start. 'So what will you do?' he asked.

'I think I'll go to Hastings. A friend of mine has been trying to get me interested in working at her estate agents. That's what I'll do. It's about time I started a proper career.'

'Sounds promising. Lots of cheap property down there, so I've heard.'

'If you need a place, you can give me a ring.'

Chris smiled. 'I will.' He stretched his arms. There was no use prolonging the conversation. 'Well, I'd better get going. I've got to see the police about that man at the YMCA. Then I'll have to find somewhere to live.'

'You'll be okay?'

'Always okay,' Chris said. 'Can I have my five hundred quid back?'

'Of course. And I'll split up the extra as well.'

'Are you sure?'

'You earned it. There'll be more because we're only splitting it two ways.' Edie stood up and left the room.

Chris climbed stiffly off the sofa and started getting dressed. Now he would have to find somewhere else for the night. He looked at his two suitcases and his box of belongings. How the hell was he going to carry all those around?

37

HALF AN HOUR later he was standing on the street, putting his belongings into a taxi. He didn't know what to say to Edie so just gave her a hug and said, 'See you in Hastings.' She waved as he climbed into the taxi. He knew he would never see her again.

'Elmhurst police station please,' he said to the driver, and then they drove away.

Chris sat in silence for the whole journey, wondering what his next move would be. He had a big bulge in his jacket pocket – just over a thousand pounds that Edie had given him – and that provided him with some comfort. But even if he found somewhere to rent, he would hardly have any money left after paying a month in advance, plus a deposit. Maybe he'd better just check into a B&B for a few days and think things through.

The taxi dropped him outside Elmhurst police station and he carried all his things inside. The policeman at the front desk smiled at him. 'Thinking of moving in?' he said. Chris told him why he was there.

A policeman came from a back room and helped him carry his suitcases down a corridor to an interview room. Then he left him alone until the door opened and another policeman came in. Chris had to laugh. It was the same policeman he'd already met twice in his flat: Larry Williamson.

'It's a small world,' Williamson said.

Chris nodded. 'We must stop meeting like this.'

Williamson looked at Chris's belongings and said, 'Having trouble finding somewhere to stay?'

'It's a long story,' Chris said.

Williamson sat down opposite. 'We picked up Dave Brill

this morning, but he denies everything you suggested on the phone. Have you got any other evidence to back up what you're saying?'

Chris had to think about that one. 'He's got a girlfriend, or ex-girlfriend, called Rosetta. She knows all about his plans to hurt me. You could ask her.'

'And where does this Rosetta live?'

'Sidcup.'

'And what's her surname?'

Chris had to think about that one as well. 'I don't know. I only met her a few times.'

Williamson shook his head and opened a notebook in front of him. 'You'd better give me the whole story from start to finish.'

Chris nodded. His stomach rumbled and his throat felt very dry. He still hadn't had any breakfast. 'Any chance of a glass of water?' he asked.

Williamson let out a deep breath and left the room.

Two hours later, Chris was standing back on the street, his two suitcases and his cardboard box next to him. The meeting with the police had not gone well, and he doubted if any charges would be brought against Dave Brill or his builder/killer friend. He felt upset and angry about it, but what could he do? If the police didn't have any proof, there was no way of charging Brill if he just denied everything. Chris thought the only thing he could do was forget about it and move on. It was no justice for Brad's death but it would make no difference to Brad. With a twinge of self-pity he thought that Edie had been right to cut him off. He was good at bringing bad luck to people.

His next problem was finding somewhere to stay for the night. He looked up and down Elmhurst High Street. He couldn't call a cab because he wouldn't know where to take it. He couldn't think of any B&Bs in the area either.

Fifty yards to his left was Sainsbury's. An idea formed in his head and he put his luggage back inside the police station, then walked over to the superstore's car park. He found an empty metal trolley and started wheeling it back to the police station. He left it in the street while he picked up his luggage. He had to put the two suitcases on their ends and force the cardboard box into the compartment nearest him. It was quite a weight to push but would have to do for now.

He felt a bit of a fool as he wheeled his possessions along. He got some funny looks from passers-by, but right now he didn't care too much. He was wearing decent clothes so he didn't look like a complete down and out – yet. He passed his old lodgings and looked up at the hole in the wall. It had a plastic sheet covering it that swayed gently in the breeze. It didn't look as though anyone would be living there for a while.

Ten minutes later, he was walking past the YMCA and he was almost tempted to check himself in. But he couldn't go back there again. He had to make a fresh start and he estimated that Rosetta's house was only another fifty minutes' walk. She had mentioned the name of the road to him once – Woolford – so he would just ask someone and then look for her Audi.

It was nearly three thirty by the time he got there. He wheeled the trolley up her drive and rang the doorbell. He was sweating from the long walk and a few miles ago he had shed his long overcoat, which was now lying on top of the trolley.

Eventually, the door opened and instead of greeting him with a big smile, Rosetta looked at him and his trolley with disgust. He knew straight away that something was wrong.

'Hello,' he said warily. 'I thought you'd be glad to see me.'

She leant on the door jam, and didn't invite him in. 'Why would I be glad to see you?'

Chris glanced at the fluffy slippers on her feet then back at her face, feeling slightly puzzled. 'Well, excuse me if I've been dreaming, but haven't we been sleeping together for the past week or so?'

Rosetta nodded. 'Yes, we have been sleeping together. But I've also discovered that you've been sleeping with someone else.'

Chris didn't know what she was talking about. 'What do you mean?'

He watched as Rosetta took a deep breath. She was wearing a turquoise sweater and blue slacks. 'On Sunday night, I came round to see you and I saw you walking into the YMCA with another woman. Cute little blonde tart, if I remember correctly.'

Chris laughed. 'I wondered what happened to you. She was a friend of mine. Her boyfriend had just died. She just came round to see me because she was upset. I remember now. A car came down the driveway that I thought I recognised. That must have been you. And I bet, in your jealousy, you rang Dave Brill and told him where I was.'

Chris didn't need to wait for an answer; he could see it in Rosetta's face. She even blushed a little.

'Well, sod you,' he said. 'Your mate Brill is now sitting in a police station waiting for the bell to toll. And as for me, I'm wheeling my belongings around in a Sainsbury's trolley.'

He didn't know what else to say. He wasn't used to outbursts of emotion. Instead, he turned the trolley around and wheeled it back on to the street. He didn't bother turning to look behind him, but he heard Rosetta closing her front door.

38

LUKE TREMBLE SPENT the whole of Sunday morning waiting for a knock on the door. He'd spent the whole of Saturday expecting the same as well. He was certain the police would be paying him a visit, but as the hours passed his confidence grew, and at one o'clock he left the flat and walked over to JD's Sportsbar and bought himself a pint of Fosters.

There were two live matches being shown in succession on Sky and he stayed there until six o'clock, knocking back eight pints and talking to a few of the regulars. Then he walked crookedly back to the flat, feeling as happy as could be expected, and passed out on his bed. Apart from two trips to the toilet, he didn't wake up until Monday morning.

Feeling hungover, he caught a train to Bexley and walked to the house they'd been working on at the end of last week, a massive four-storey Victorian construction. When he arrived, there was no sign of Dave or the Toyota Hiace, so he sat in the garden, wondering what to do. It was a mild, overcast day, and he read the *Sun* from cover to cover. By midday, though, he was getting restless, so he left the garden and went to find a telephone box.

He found one a few hundred yards away, stepped inside and rang Dave's mobile. All he got was a message saying the mobile had been turned off. He dialed Dave's home number and after a few rings his wife, Evelyn, picked it up.

'Uh, hello,' he said. 'It's Luke. I was wondering where Dave was today.'

There was a pause at the end of the line and then a sigh. 'Dave's at the police station. He's been there all morning. I don't suppose you know why? He's not telling me a thing.'

Alarm bells started ringing in Luke's head. 'Uh, no,' he said quickly. 'Haven't got a clue.'

'He says it's a case of mistaken identity. He never came home last night and then he rang this morning. Something's wrong but I don't know what.'

Luke didn't know what to say. 'Well, I'd better go home then. I can't do a thing on my own.'

'Ring this evening. Hopefully he'll be home by then.'

Luke put the phone down and walked back to the house for his bag. Now he was really worried. Why the hell was Dave at the police station? Had that Chris Small fellow turned him in? Now it would only be a matter of time before they came for him. He wondered whether he should go home or not. Maybe they'd be waiting for him already.

When he got to the house he saw that the owner was standing in the front garden, looking up at the roof. She was a middle-aged woman with a purple, granny hairdo. He nodded at her as he walked up the drive and she looked at him sternly.

'I wondered where you'd got to,' she said. 'I can't get a decent picture on my TV. It's been really bad all weekend. What did you do to it?'

Luke looked up at the roof. 'We had to move the aerial a bit, on Friday. There was no one in so we couldn't test it. I'll go up and fix it if you like.'

'I'd be grateful if you could. I'm missing Richard and Judy.'

Luke didn't know who Richard and Judy were. 'I'll go and fiddle with it. You'll have to come out and tell me when it's okay.'

'All right,' said the woman, disappearing inside.

Luke walked to the tower scaffolding and started climbing up. He'd fix the aerial and then go home. He'd have a good look for police cars before entering his building, though. And then maybe he'd ask Dave for a few weeks' holiday. Disappear until the whole thing died down.

When he reached the roof he had to climb over the tiles to the chimney. They were old and covered with moss, making them slippery and awkward.

The TV aerial was attached to the top of the chimney and

Luke started twisting it in the direction he thought it had been originally. Then he waited for the woman to come out. She didn't make an appearance so he started twisting it some more. After about five minutes, she came out and shouted up at him.

'That's okay! Thanks very much!'

Luke saluted her and was about to start his descent when he heard police sirens. He stopped for a second to listen and they were definitely getting louder, obviously heading in his direction. He turned around quickly, looking for the easiest way down, but when he stepped on a tile his foot slipped on some moss and he started sliding down the roof on his backside. Before he could grab anything he was over the edge, then his right foot got caught in the scaffolding and flipped him over. He screamed as he went through the air and landed, head-first, on the concrete below.

As he lay there in a crumpled heap, with the life slowly oozing out of him, he heard the police cars getting louder and then fading into the distance. They hadn't been coming for him after all.

After leaving Rosetta's, Chris spent the rest of the afternoon trying to find somewhere to stay. He wheeled his trolley around the streets of Sidcup but couldn't find a single place. And then it started to rain.

He put his coat back on, but now his luggage was exposed to the elements. He started wheeling the trolley faster in the direction of Elmhurst, knowing he would once again have to check into the YMCA. It was the only place he could think of, and at least they knew his face and wouldn't turn him away.

As he was approaching the A20 flyover there was a sudden squall of rain and the wind started blowing harder. He stopped the trolley, took off his luggage, and dropped it on the other side of the fence. Then he climbed over and started carrying his things down the steep bank and under the bridge. Traffic was speeding by underneath and he had to make two trips. When he sat down in the dry, he was out of breath and soaked to the skin.

The cardboard box looked like it was about to collapse, so he started taking stuff out and cramming the essentials into the two suitcases. When he'd finished, the cases were packed solid and would be very heavy to carry, but at least there were only two things to lift. The rest of the contents from the box he would leave under the bridge for the first hobo or motorway maintenance man to find. There were a few books, a pair of trainers, some old T-shirts, and all of his cutlery, plates, glasses and mugs.

He looked out at the weather but it seemed to be getting worse and soon it would be getting dark. He munched on a Twix and drank from a small bottle of mineral water.

He sat and thought things through, wondering how his life had got to this stage. Was it all bad luck or did he just bring it on himself? It was something he'd have to find the answer to or he could end up a down-and-out. He watched the rainfall as the headlights of the passing cars got brighter.

39

EXACTLY TWENTY-FOUR hours after being arrested, Dave Brill was released and allowed back on the streets of Elmhurst. He felt extremely tired after a restless night in his cell, and the first thing he did was ring Evelyn on his mobile.

'So they've set you free,' she said, a slight trace of sarcasm in her voice.

'As I told you, it was a case of mistaken identity,' he lied.

'You'll have to tell me about it later, but first of all you should know that Luke died yesterday.'

Brill stood, frozen to the spot, and said, 'You what?'

'Yesterday, Luke fell from the roof you were working on. I got a phone call from the woman who lives there. He'd been trying to fix her TV aerial and fell off.'

Brill didn't know what to say. 'Fucking hell,' was all he could manage.

'So now you'll have to find a new worker. The police want to talk to you as well. I hope your scaffolding was safe.'

'Of course it was safe,' he said sharply. 'It's always safe. Luke must've done something stupid.'

'Well, we can talk about it later.'

'Yeah. I've got to go and get my car first.' Then he shut off the mobile and started walking towards the YMCA.

He had never known anyone quite like Luke, and in a strange way he would miss him. Although he was a bit thick and could act like a nutter, he was a good worker and pretty reliable. How the hell had he managed to fall off the roof? Brill had never had any close escapes in his whole building career, although it was something he often thought about; falling from a roof was one of his secret fears and he shuddered to think of it happening to him.

At least the police hadn't been able to charge him with anything so far. That was one good thing to think about. He'd replied with 'No comment,' to all of their questions, on the advice of his solicitor. No doubt a sizeable bill would soon be coming his way for that little piece of wisdom.

It took ten minutes to walk to the YMCA. It was a fresh morning after a night of heavy rain; the grass on the verge was still damp and puddles lay by the side of the road. After picking up the car, he would go home and take the rest of the day off. He had two nights of sleep to catch up on. He still felt humiliated by his night in the YMCA with his mobile stuck in his mouth, occasionally playing 'Land Of Hope And Glory'. He would like to beat the shit out of Small for that little trick but he supposed there was no way he'd find him now. He was probably out of his hands forever. He would have to forget the whole thing and just carry on with his life. A life with no Rosetta as well.

Brill walked down the front drive of the YMCA, towards the large car park behind the main building. When he'd come to see Small on Sunday he'd parked the BMW at the rear, as far away from the building as possible. He turned towards the tarmac, winding his way through parked cars, until eventually the BMW came into view. He had to look twice to make sure it really was his vehicle. Then he started screaming and swearing out loud.

From a window on the second floor of the YMCA, Chris watched Dave Brill's reaction and smiled. At last he had hit the bastard where it really hurt. He watched him run over to the BMW and collapse on the ground next to it. Then he started beating the tarmac with his fist. Chris had never seen anyone do that before, except in comedy films. Maybe there was some justice in the world after all.

Then Brill stood up and started walking towards the YMCA. Chris stood back from the window. No doubt Brill would ask at reception what the hell had happened, but that would get him nowhere. No one had seen Chris in action in the early hours of the morning.

Sitting under the bridge yesterday evening, Chris had suddenly thought about Brill's car and how it was probably still at the YMCA. The police would have told him to leave it behind when they'd picked him up on Monday morning. The thought had forced Chris out of his dry hiding place and back into the rain.

He had struggled with his two suitcases up the steep motorway bank, put them back in the shopping trolley, then wheeled it over the bridge. He had walked the remaining mile to the YMCA, dumped the trolley at the entrance, and entered the building soaked through and whacked. He'd asked for a room at the back, overlooking the car park.

After changing into some dry clothes Chris walked into the car park to see if Brill's car was still there. He smiled with pleasure when he saw it, the two scratches still down both sides. After borrowing an umbrella from reception, he walked to a pub in the old part of Elmhurst and drank two whiskies and a pint of bitter to warm himself up. Then he went to the local 24-hour garage, where he purchased a red plastic gallon can and filled it with petrol. On his way back to the YMCA, he bought a Chinese takeaway and ate it in his room.

He waited until two in the morning, playing blackjack on the laptop that was luckily still working. Then he left the YMCA by an emergency exit, propping the door open with a piece of cardboard.

He walked over to the BMW, and, making sure no one was watching, poured petrol all over it, then a thin line on the ground a safe distance away. He hid the can in some nearby dustbins, then threw a match on the ground and watched the flames rush over to the BMW. He was back in the YMCA when he heard it explode. Then residents started popping their heads out of doors to see what was going on.

Back in his room, Chris watched the fire engines arrive and aim their hoses at the flames. A crowd had gathered to watch;

the YMCA clientele in their dressing gowns and slippers. Chris stripped off and fell exhausted into bed. He watched the flames making patterns on his walls until eventually they disappeared.

40

CHRIS WAITED AN hour or so to make sure Dave Brill
wasn't still on the premises, then left his room and walked
down to reception. He rang the police from the payphone and
asked for Larry Williamson. He told the policeman that he'd
remembered Rosetta's address and she could confirm his story.
He knew Rosetta would hate talking to the police but that was
tough shit. Larry said he would check it out. Maybe this time
they would get something to pin on Brill.

Chris decided to go for a walk. He would lie low for a
couple of days and think about his future. He walked the half
mile to Elmhurst pond and sat on a bench. He looked at the
dirty water and the ducks, and glanced over the road at his old
lodgings. He thought of Edie and wondered how she'd get on
in Hastings. He smiled when he thought of her optimism, back
when they'd first formed their blackjack team. She'd been so
sure they were on to a winner. He supposed it was a good idea
at the time, and without Brill's intervention, who knows where
it would have led. They could have ended up with a couple of
grand each, or more.

Then he thought about his list of life achievements and
realised it was now down to just two things.

1. He was still alive; and

2. He had about fifteen hundred pounds to his name plus
his flat deposit, whenever that arrived.

He thought about Brad and the wasteful end to his short
life. Then he realised, as if someone had just turned a light on
in his head, that as long as he was still alive there would always
be hope; if he was dead like Brad then there was no hope at all.

He was glad he hadn't seen Brad's corpse. Although he had
seen him lying unconscious on Oxford Street, at least he had

still been alive, and he knew it was totally different to seeing a dead body. He would prefer to remember Brad as the friendly, good-natured American that he was, and not as some grey, cold, lifeless form lying in the morgue.

He got up from the bench and started walking towards Sainsbury's. He would buy some lunch and take it back to his room. Maybe he could find someone to have a game of snooker with, back at the YMCA.

There was a young man standing outside Sainsbury's selling *The Big Issue*. Chris occasionally bought the magazine in London but generally ignored the sellers. Most of them were young and looked intelligent enough to find themselves a job. He thought any job must be better than standing on a street corner, begging people for money. He couldn't understand the mentality behind it. He decided to ignore this seller, a man in his twenties with long hair and stubble.

As he was walking past the seller though, the man said to him, 'Buy the Big Issue. Help the homeless.'

Chris shook his head and said, 'At least you're still alive.'

The seller gave him a funny look.

Chris picked up a shopping basket and started walking around. He wandered down the aisles looking at all the packets of frozen food, the ready-made microwave meals, the best-selling CDs and books, and horrendous men's magazines; all pre-packaged junk for a lazy and pampered society. He scanned the bestselling videos and came to the realisation that Brad was right; most of them were entertainment for the brain-dead. Then he looked with distaste at the overweight housewives wheeling their shopping carts, filled to the brim. How did people manage to eat so much? Then he started thinking about Brad again and decided to leave.

He put his basket back by the front door and walked out. He stopped next to the Big Issue seller and reached in his pocket. The seller looked at him with surprise.

'Too crowded,' Chris said. 'I'll have one of your magazines please.'

The seller handed one over and Chris gave him a couple of quid. 'Keep the change,' he said.

'Thanks,' said the seller. He nodded towards the supermarket and said, 'They don't know how lucky they are, do they?'

Chris smiled at him. 'No they don't.' And then he walked away.

He started heading back towards the YMCA, but as he was passing The Pilgrim's Rest, decided to go in for a pint instead. He walked up the side road next to his old lodgings, pushed open the door and entered.

He bought a pint of bitter and sat next to the window. He looked across the road at the rickety wooden gate where the large policeman had been standing a few months ago, waiting to tell him he'd been robbed. So much had happened since.

Chris took off his coat and felt something in the inside pocket. He reached in and found his small pack of cards and, much to his amazement, one of Edie's numbered cards with The Main Count strategy printed on it. Now how the hell had that got there? He tried thinking back but was pretty sure she'd never given it to him. He sat there puzzled for a while and all he could think was that she'd slipped it into his pocket that night he'd stayed at her flat. Maybe she was trying to tell him something. Maybe this was her way of saying it was time he learnt how to count cards.

He propped The Main Count table against his pint glass, took the cards out of the packet and shuffled them. Then he started dealing them face up, looking at The Main Count, trying to keep a running total. He remembered that Edie had said his score should be zero when all the cards had been dealt. About five minutes later, the cards were finished and his count was minus two. That wasn't too bad. Only two out, but he would have to be a lot faster as well. He tried remembering what she'd told him about speed. Was it something like thirty seconds for the whole pack? That seemed unreasonably fast. He reckoned a minute would be fast enough.

He picked up the cards again, pressed a few buttons on his

wristwatch, then started the stopwatch and timed himself. Four minutes and fifty-five seconds later he had finished, this time with a running count of plus three. Not too bad, not too good. It would obviously take a lot of practice but he could feel the excitement welling up inside him. He thought back to Sunday and his large winnings with Basic Strategy. If he could master this counting lark as well, the possibilities were endless. He had no job to tie him down so he could spend long hours in casinos, perfecting his art. He could rent a flat somewhere in London and become a professional gambler! The whole idea made perfect sense. He started smiling. Who would have thought it would come to this?

He finished his pint quickly, gathered up his things, and left the pub. He would go back to his room, turn on his laptop, and check out the counting system on his computer program. Then he would start putting in the hours, the hours that could change his life. He thought about his new image: Chris Small – professional gambler. Something about it sounded just right.